The missing side of the triangle

The missing side of the triangle

Assessing the importance of family and
environmental factors in the lives of children

Gordon Jack and Owen Gill

Barnardo's
GIVING CHILDREN BACK THEIR FUTURE

Barnardo's vision is that the lives of all children and young people should be free from poverty, abuse and discrimination.

Barnardo's purpose is to help the most vulnerable children and young people transform their lives and fulfil their potential.

© Barnardo's 2003

All rights reserved. No part of this publication may be reproduced, stored on a retrieval system or transmitted in any form or by any means without permission of the publisher.

First published in 2003 by Barnardo's

Barnardo's, Tanners Lane, Barkingside, Iford, Essex IG6 1QG

Charity registration number 216250

A catalogue record for this book is available from the British Library

ISBN 0 902046 93 4

This publication is available in other formats on request

Acknowledgements

The authors have benefited from the advice of a number of people at various stages in the writing of this book. Nigel Parton, Helen Roberts, Peter Fanshawe, Liza Bingley Miller, Alan Coombe, Julie Skorupka, Anne Goymer and Jon Doble provided us with very valuable feedback.

Barnardo's anti-poverty work in the South West is supported by the Lloyds TSB Foundation for England and Wales.

Throughout this book, we have used anonymised practice examples to illustrate the interactions between different dimensions of the Assessment Framework.

Contents

			Page
Chapter	1	Introduction	1
	2	Community resources	9
	3	Social integration	31
	4	Income	53
	5	Employment	69
	6	Housing	85
	7	Wider family	103
	8	Family history and functioning	121
	9	Implementing the framework	139
Appendix	1	Areas for assessment in relation to the impact of family and environmental factors on the lives of children	149
Appendix	2	A model for assessing the impact of 'community' on parents and children	161
Index of authors cited			163

CHILD'S DEVELOPMENTAL NEEDS

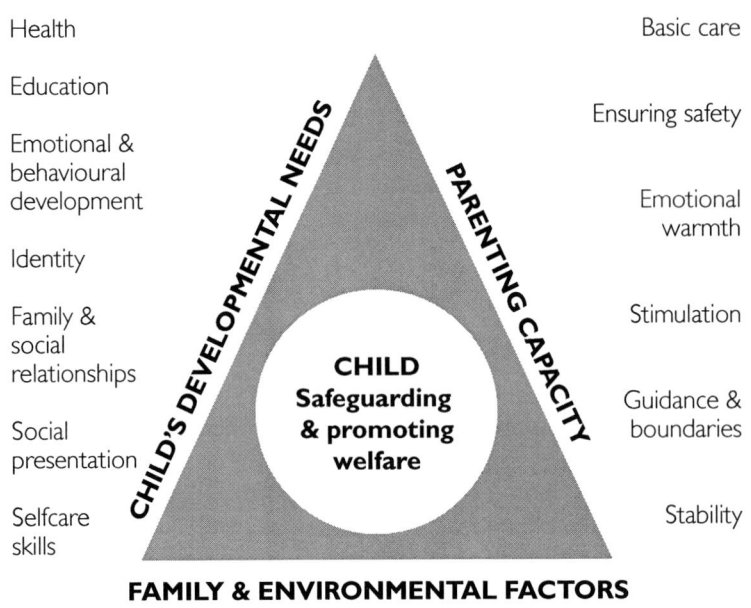

- Health
- Education
- Emotional & behavioural development
- Identity
- Family & social relationships
- Social presentation
- Selfcare skills

PARENTING CAPACITY

- Basic care
- Ensuring safety
- Emotional warmth
- Stimulation
- Guidance & boundaries
- Stability

CHILD Safeguarding & promoting welfare

FAMILY & ENVIRONMENTAL FACTORS

- Community resources
- Family's social integration
- Income
- Employment
- Housing
- Wider family
- Family history & functioning

Introduction

This book has three aims. The first is to provide a review of the research evidence relevant to a full understanding of the ecological approach to child and family assessment. The second is to relate this body of knowledge to practice situations that will be familiar to child welfare practitioners in the UK. The third is to provide tools to assist practitioners in their assessments of the interactions between external environmental factors and the internal world of the family.

Background

As part of the Quality Protects programme, designed to improve children's services, the government has produced guidance, practice materials and training resources on the assessment of children in need and their families. The Assessment Framework (Department of Health, 2000a) presents the variables to be taken into consideration in the form of a triangle, with the three sides representing the interacting domains of children's developmental needs, parenting capacity, and wider family and environmental factors. The framework therefore adopts an ecological model, within which the development of children is understood to be inextricably linked to the characteristics of the environments that they inhabit (Bronfenbrenner, 1979; Jack and Jack, 2000).

Effective implementation of the framework, as John Hutton, the Minister responsible, has acknowledged, requires detailed knowledge and understanding (Department of Health, 2000b). This includes understanding of the principles underpinning the ecological approach itself, and knowledge of the research evidence concerning the mutual interactions between different aspects of children's development, parenting capacity and the wider environments that they inhabit. There is now a considerable body of knowledge and expertise about the assessment of the internal dynamics of families, much of which has helpfully been made available to accompany the Assessment Framework. However, the same cannot be said about the ways in which these internal factors interact with the child's wider family, community, and culture. This book is an attempt to redress the balance and to fill some of the important gaps in knowledge and thinking that we have identified.

Internal and external pressures on families

Over the past 25 years, UK child and family welfare policy and practice have often ignored the wider family, community and structural dimensions of family life – or at least relegated them to a position of very limited importance. There are a number of reasons for this, the most important of which is undoubtedly the political context, in which there was a failure to acknowledge the impact of community and structural factors, particularly poverty and its accompanying inequalities, on family life and the welfare of children (Jack and Jack, 2000). In this wider political environment, child welfare organisations and professional interest and expertise in the UK developed with a primary focus on the increasingly sophisticated interpretation of internal family relationships. The influence of developments in family therapy, for instance, was very significant during this period in supporting interpersonal definitions of family difficulties. There is also a lack of a strong research tradition in the UK that examines the connections between external community and structural factors and what happens within families.

However, there are a number of significant ways in which the political climate in the UK has changed in recent years, leading to a greater focus on the structural and community influences on parents and children. It has been acknowledged that very high levels of child poverty, and other inequalities in the areas of health, employment, housing, childcare, and transport all seriously undermine the future life chances of large numbers of the UK population. Also, to enable the UK to compete effectively in a globalised economy, the government is now having to consider ways of improving the levels of education and skills of the population. A number of social policy measures have been introduced to improve the quality of education and training provided in schools and colleges, and attention has been given to a wider social inclusion agenda. As a result, a great deal of government spending and social policy is now directed towards reducing structural inequalities and improving the communities in which children in need and their families live. We will examine these developments in some detail, but the important point to note here is that this social inclusion agenda, and the political context in which it has emerged, is also responsible for the ecological approach that underpins the Assessment Framework.

The ecological approach: implications for practice

In our view, the ecological principles that underpin the Assessment Framework offer child welfare practitioners and their employing organisations an opportunity to develop practice that is more in tune with families' own perceptions and interpretations of their difficulties. Many families, in our experience, already provide relatively sophisticated ecological interpretations of their difficulties, which demonstrate a more complete awareness of the influence of external pressures and constraints on what happens within their families than is often officially acknowledged by the welfare agencies with which they are in contact.

These differing perspectives can cause serious problems in any attempts to find agreed solutions to difficult family problems, as is illustrated by the following description of a case conference attended by one of the authors.

> The conference was convened to consider the alleged neglect by John and Laura Grant of their two children. The workers involved perceived the difficulties to be the result of parental inadequacies and the breakdown of relationships within the family. John Grant's view was that the cause of problems within the family was a lack of sufficient household income and the harassment of family members by neighbours. Notwithstanding these different perceptions, the first 30 minutes of the conference were taken up by the professionals discussing the family purely in terms of the personal difficulties the parents had in caring satisfactorily for the children and the neglect that the children were experiencing as a result. Both parents remained very quiet during this discussion. Finally, Mr. Grant smashed his fist hard into the case conference table and shouted, *'How would you like to live on the money I get every week?'*

One of the potential strengths of the ecological approach is that it encourages workers to pay full heed to people's own definitions and interpretations of their circumstances, so helping to minimise the risk of differences in perspective.

The ecological approach also makes it possible for practitioners and managers to more effectively highlight and influence the structural and community factors that are having a negative impact on parenting capacity and child development. For example, the new assessment categories help to reveal connections between factors, such as particular areas of residence, types of housing, and levels of community resources, that make the task of parenting difficult for anybody, let alone parents who come to disadvantaged environments with significant personal problems of their own. The key to successful ecological assessments will often lie in the worker's ability to listen to what family members are saying about their overall circumstances, and to help them to identify their strengths and difficulties and the webs of causation, association and mutual influence.

The ecological approach also demands that workers are familiar with the communities in which the children and families they are working with are living. Workers can make accurate assessments of a family's level of social integration or use of community resources, for instance, only if they are familiar with the nature of the community involved, including its strengths as well as its weaknesses. Many social services departments and statutory health and education services are currently organised largely on deficit models and individual referrals. The ecological approach requires a more social or community perspective, that involves assessing the needs of vulnerable groups and developing responses to pressures on families and children that provide a significant preventive component.

This is consistent with the approach advocated within the Sure Start and Children's Fund programmes, which have community provision and involvement at their heart.

This approach also involves workers and their employing agencies acquiring better knowledge of one another's services and developing joint working arrangements in local areas.

Finally, this 'wide-angled' view also needs to encompass an understanding of the cultures in which people live and a willingness to explore the way that these cultures can influence behaviour and attitudes within families. In this context 'culture' is a broad concept that includes important and interrelated aspects of religion, history, class and ethnicity, for example, but that can also refer to much more local issues, such as the prevailing atmosphere within a particular block of flats or group of adjacent streets.

The 'missing' side of the triangle

The Assessment Framework potentially offers agencies and workers new ways of relating to children and families and new ways of understanding the pressures they experience. However, it is difficult to locate research and practice evidence on which to base an ecological assessment. Nearly all of the resources published to accompany the Assessment Framework reflect and reassert internal interpretations of family difficulties. Very little material addresses directly the influence of wider family and environmental factors on families, never mind going on to examine how these factors interact with one another and with the different dimensions of children's development and parenting capacity. For example, the reader produced to accompany the Assessment Framework (Horwath, 2001) consists of four parts: the first two cover the framework itself, and the general assessment process, and the other two sections go on to deal with the first two sides of the assessment triangle (children's developmental needs and parenting capacity) only. There is no section covering the third side of the triangle (wider family and environmental factors) and the only significant mention of these issues is confined to individual chapters by Jack and Gilligan.

The lack of material on structural and community influences on families is repeated in the pack of questionnaires and scales that accompany the Assessment Framework. Helpful as these new assessment tools are, they focus on issues related to the internal dynamics of families and largely fail to address the family's surrounding environment. Finally, the core assessment forms provided to record assessments also emphasise the importance of factors within families, to the detriment of external influences. The first 14 pages of the assessment section of the forms are devoted to recording information about the seven dimensions of child development, alongside the six dimensions of parenting capacity. This way of recording the information is adopted to ensure that the interactions between different aspects of these two sides of the assessment triangle are considered.

However, the seven dimensions on the third side of the triangle, covering wider family and environmental influences on parents and children, are confined to three pages, after the rest of the assessment information has been recorded. Furthermore, workers are asked only to record the way that wider family and environmental factors influence child development and parenting capacity and not to record mutual influences. Using such a uni-directional approach does not, for example, allow workers to record the way in which the individual characteristics of both children and parents help to shape the social environments that they inhabit. This is a fundamental aspect of the ecological approach.

Any consideration of the mutual interactions between wider family and environmental factors and different aspects of child development and parenting capacity is therefore unlikely to be incorporated into assessments that rely on the government forms, or local recording arrangements derived from them. This is especially worrying because the early indications, from the government-commissioned evaluation of the implementation of the new Assessment Framework, are that the analysis of the information being collected is currently very poor (Cleaver, 2002).

It is for these reasons that we have entitled this volume, focused on the wider family and environmental influences on children in need and their families, the 'missing' side of the triangle.

Structure of the book

The book is intended to be of use to anyone involved in any way with assessments of children in need and their families. This includes practitioners, managers, policy makers, students, parents/carers and young people.

The structure of the book follows the seven dimensions of the 'Wider family and environmental factors' side of the government's Assessment Framework: community resources, social integration, income, employment, housing, family history and functioning, and wider family. Issues affecting particular groups, such as different minority ethnic communities and children or parents with disabilities, are integrated into each of the chapters. Anonymised practice examples are also used throughout the book, to illustrate the interactions between different dimensions of the Assessment Framework in people's lives

This structure was adopted to make it easier for readers, most of whom will already be familiar with the Assessment Framework, to find their way around the book and to use it to inform their decision-making in practice. However, as the main principle underlying our approach (and that of the Assessment Framework itself) is that of an integrated, ecological perspective, we accept that there are dangers in compartmentalising the separate dimensions in this way. To address this problem, each chapter highlights the main interactions with other dimensions in the triangle and concludes with a section identifying the main issues for assessments. In the concluding chapter, we draw out the main messages for assessments, policy formulation and service delivery that emerge from the research evidence and practice examples presented in the book. The appendices offer practice tools, drawn from our review of the research literature, to assist practitioners to identify key links between different dimensions within the Assessment Framework. These tools should not be used as yet another checklist, to be inflicted on every family who is involved in an assessment. Rather, they are intended to help in making appropriate connections between the internal and external factors affecting families, and to point the way to more appropriate and effective ways of meeting any needs identified.

References

Bronfenbrenner, U (1979) *The Ecology of Human Development*. Cambridge: Harvard University Press

Cleaver, H (2002) Department of Health Seminar on *The Integrated Children's System*. London (March)

Department of Health (2000a) *Framework for the Assessment of Children in Need and their Families*. London: The Stationery Office

Department of Health (2000b) *Assessing Children in Need and their Families: Practice guidance*. London: The Stationery Office

Horwath, J (ed) (2001) *The Child's World: Assessing children in need. The reader.* London: Jessica Kingsley

Jack, G and Jack, D (2000) Ecological Social Work: The application of a systems model of development in context.. In P Stepney and D Ford (eds) *Social Work Models, Methods and Theories: A framework for practice*, pp93–104. Lyme Regis: Russell House

Community resources 2

The term 'community resources' can be conceptualised in two ways. First it can refer to all the systems of help, support, advice, guidance, and general activities in the local area to which families have access. Secondly, it can refer to the 'social capital' within the community and include all of the informal contacts and networks of which the child and the family are a part. There are therefore strong connections between *community resources* and the other assessment categories within the framework. There is, for instance, a strong link between community resources and *social integration*: the level of resources that a community has for contact and the development of support will have a direct impact on the level of social integration.

Children's and parents' own definition of 'community'

Before we look at the range and impact of different aspects of community resources, it is important to point out that the term 'community' can cause confusion in assessing the world of the child and the parent. First there is a danger that assumptions about where communities begin and end may be based on the administrative and 'official' boundaries of particular communities, rather than on the views and perceptions of children and parents.

The second danger is that the term 'community' carries with it assumptions not only about how children and families live, but also about how they ought to live. It tends to convey ideas about the ideal or the potential of human relationships. So, in assessing community resources, it is important to recognise that for parents and children, community resources can be both positive and negative. The resources that a community has may bring great benefits but their lack, or their particular characteristics, may also bring dangers and difficulties for children and families (Williams, 1993; Gilroy, 1987).

In adopting a definition of 'community' it is therefore important to start from the perspectives of the child and family. For some children and families the notion of community will be one which is constrained geographically.

The lone parent who does not work outside the home, has very limited financial resources and no means of private transport, may realistically see her or his immediate geographical 'community' as the only one that is relevant because this is the only one to which she or he has access.

For other children and families a different definition may be appropriate. Asylum-seeking families, for instance, will in all probability relate not to a temporary residence which has been allocated to them but to a collection of loyalties, interests, and identities which may bear little relationship to that residence. Equally, black children and parents living on primarily white estates may relate far more readily to a geographically dispersed community.

The incorporation of the idea of community resources into the ecological model invites not only an assessment of the impact of these resources on the child and family from the perspective of the resource provider but also – equally importantly – it invites an assessment of the child's and the family's perceptions of these resources. This goes to the heart of the ecological perspective in terms of child and family assessment. Rather than being seen simply as being moulded by their circumstances and the resources that are available to them, children and families are seen to be in a constant state of interaction with the social and organisational world around them.

Differing perceptions of 'community' within families

Parents' perspectives on community may differ markedly from those of children. The parents may see the community as having a number of resources that are relevant to them and support them in their task of being a parent. However, the child, particularly the older child, may perceive the community as lacking in resources that make life sustainable for someone of his or her age. The resources that children can access in their communities will obviously be related to the resources that their parents can access, but some will be specifically relevant to children and must be given separate attention.

It is also important to distinguish between those resources which are available to men and those which are available for women. For instance, the local 'community' might have significant resources of support and social contact for women but far fewer for men – or vice versa. The level and nature of resources for different family members may have a significant impact on how they perform their role as parents. The presence or lack of activities for men, for instance, may have a significant bearing on how they engage in their role as fathers to their children.

The crucial point is that there is not just one 'community' with one set of community resources. There will be as many different communities as there are family members, and assessments need to incorporate these different perspectives.

Accessibility

The accessibility of community resources can be as important as their availability. Accessibility can be analysed in a number of ways.

First there is the question of whether the resource has the capacity to be available to all of the children and parents who may wish or need to use it. For instance, a local child guidance service may have skilled workers and their interventions may be effective but their waiting lists may be so long that accessibility is low. Or, in more informal community resources, there may be local clubs for children but these may be oversubscribed, resulting in low accessibility.

It is also important to consider whether or not the resource is physically accessible to those who need to make use of it. This will be important for all parents but especially for those who are living on low incomes and who may not have their own transport. Accessibility will be a particular issue for many families living in rural areas, although the general levels of disadvantage may be less extreme than in some urban areas.

This is well illustrated by the publication in recent years of the Department of Environment, Transport and the Regions indicators of multiple deprivation (DETR, 2000). These indicators look at disadvantage on a number of dimensions, including employment and child poverty. So, for instance, a rural area may not have wards in the top range of disadvantage but it may have wards which are in the top range for lack of accessibility to services.

Cost will also influence accessibility. The chapter on income in this volume shows, for example, that the costs of daycare for children in the UK, are the highest in Europe, placing this essential resource beyond the reach of many parents, despite the financial help provided by the government through tax credits.

Accessibility will also be an important issue for particular groups of parents and children. For example, because of the association between disability and poverty, children with disabilities will be particularly dependent on local community resources. Approximately 3 per cent of children in the UK have a disability (Sharma, 2002). Of all the families in the UK who care for children with disability, 55 per cent either are or have been living in poverty. Children with disabilities are also far more likely to be born into poorer families. Children are three times more likely to have a disability if their father is an unskilled manual worker as opposed to a professional (Gordon, Parker and Loughron, 2000).

Research also shows that some community resources may not be available to and accessible for families from minority ethnic groups. For instance, a study by Ravinda Barn and her colleagues (Barn, Sinclair and Ferdinand, 1997) showed the very low level of self-referrals to social services from Asian families. Another study (Qureshi, Berridge and Wenman, 2000) looked at the availability and perceived effectiveness of support services for South Asian families, and found that a low level of services was being provided to meet their needs and that self-referrals were rare. Qureshi and colleagues found that, among the families they interviewed, 'there was a general lack of awareness … of the role of social services and availability of family support.' (p54).

These examples illustrate that the use made of community resources depends, in large measure, on how they are perceived by the families that might benefit from them. Some resources may be perceived by families as stigmatising and so will be little used. Practice experience, for example, indicates a low take-up of some parenting classes in local communities for this reason. Informal neighbourhood social groups (for instance at community or family centres) may give the impression that they are open only to an established 'clique' of existing members. At a more general level, services and service locations may be inaccessible to vulnerable families because of poor publicity or because it takes social skills to access the services. For instance, local family centres may offer a range of informal group activities but they may be used primarily by people with more developed social networks and higher social skills.

Demographic composition of individual communities

In assessing community resources it is also important to analyse the demographic composition of the local area. High levels of collective need and a lack of resources and facilities in the community can be a major stress factor for families.

It is also important to consider the rate of mobility into and out of the area. In areas with high levels of mobility there may be attendant 'social disorganisation', leading potentially to a lack of clear cultural norms and social support around childcare (see, for instance, Garbarino and Crouter, 1978).

It will also be important to ask whether the community is 'balanced' or if there are a disproportionate number of people of particular age groups, or those experiencing particular pressures such as lone parents or families on very low income. In the UK, Burrows (1997) has drawn attention to the changing age structure in the most disadvantaged communities living in the social rented sector. He shows that these communities are characterised by a disproportionate number of young single people and young families.

Safety as a community resource

Workers also need to consider whether residents perceive the community as a place which is safe or dangerous. Issues for parents and children will include:

- physical danger in the local environment: dangerous buildings, water, and dangerous play areas
- road danger: road accidents continue to be the highest cause of death for children, and these are more likely to occur in disadvantaged areas; in 2001, 4,968 children were killed or seriously injured on British roads (Department of Transport, 2002)
- people danger: people in the area outside the family who parents and children consider to be a threat to children
- drugs danger: a current feature of many disadvantaged areas is the fear of drugs, on the part of both parents and children.

Safety can also be thought of in more positive terms, in the sense of protective factors in the community. These protective factors include people outside the family to whom a child might go if they are frightened or anxious. They would also include a general culture in the area of 'people looking out for other people's children'. Whilst these factors are difficult to quantify, they are an important element in community resources for children.

Community resources for parents

Some resources may be available and potentially accessible to all groups within the community, while others will be restricted to people of a particular background, age or location. Still others will be restricted to people who have been defined by welfare professionals in a particular way.

Any categorisation of resources is, to some extent, arbitrary. However, the following areas of categorisation will be of importance for those doing family assessments.

Family support services

Defining family support as 'Any activity or facility provided either by statutory agencies or by community groups or individuals, aimed at providing advice and support to parents to help them in bringing up their children' (Audit Commission, 1994), reveals the very broad range of services that can be included under this heading. We have found it helpful to separate these services into: formal, semi-formal and informal services and list below some of the main community resources that may be available under these three categories.

Formal family support services

- Local social services support (eg social work visits)
- Structured individual or group support (eg from a family or resource or health centre base)
- Structured support from health services (eg health visitor)

Semi-formal family support services

- Parenting classes
- Groups geared towards particular parenting activities, such as cooking

- Men's or women's groups (eg Newpin groups or father's groups in a family centre)
- Home-visiting by a volunteer (eg Homestart)
- Parent support groups run by social services or family centres
- Sure Start support groups (eg breastfeeding groups)
- Groups for parents with specific childcare needs, such as parents of disabled children

Informal family support services

- Drop-in groups run by family centres, health centres, social services and voluntary groups
- Neighbourhood groups focusing on, for example, children's health and safety issues

The above list is far from exhaustive. In fact, difficulties can arise for families because of the complexity and the range of agencies, groups and individuals who might be involved in their local area. Services are also often in a state of flux, with new facilities regularly emerging and others closing down. This highlights how important it is for professionals to be familiar with what is currently available in the local communities in which they work, what the existing services are designed to provide, and how they can be accessed.

The effectiveness of many of these services, both in terms of reaching those most in need, and in terms of improved outcomes for parents and children, is increasingly being examined by specific research studies and systematic reviews of the research literature (eg Statham, 2000; Macdonald and Roberts, 1995; Beresford et al, 1996; Roberts, 2000; Macdonald with Winkley, 1999). For example, group-based parenting programmes, using behavioural approaches that help parents to use positive reinforcement techniques effectively, have been shown to be capable of achieving long-term improvements in the behaviour of pre-adolescent children. Alternatively, programmes that emphasise communication and relationships have been found to be more effective in improving outcomes for parents, including reducing family conflict and increasing family cohesion (Lloyd, 1999). Parents attending a wide range of programmes generally report high levels of satisfaction, especially when the group leaders are parents themselves (Grimshaw and McGuire,

1998). However, on the down side, parenting programmes have not been so effective at involving fathers or parents from minority ethnic groups (Smith and Pugh, 1996), These problems are shared by many services designed to provide family support, including many family centres, and respite care services (Ghate, Shaw and Hazel, 2000; Singh, 1992).

Anti-poverty facilities

All of the evidence is that families of children 'in need' are likely to be overwhelmingly from poorer groups in society. This is underlined by the findings from 24 studies, commissioned by the Department of Health, into how the Children Act 1989 is working in England and Wales (Aldgate and Statham, 2001). For example, 98 per cent of the families whose children were at risk of suffering emotional maltreatment or neglect in one of the studies were characterised by the extreme poverty of their material environment (Thoburn, Wilding and Watson, 2000).

At the most direct level, there is therefore a need for an assessment of whether the basic necessities of life are available, at affordable prices, in the local area. The existence of good-quality cheap food will be an essential part of the analysis. Poorer families often lack their own transport, making it very difficult for them to access the cheaper, but usually more distant, supermarkets and forcing them into a dependence on higher-priced local shops.

It is also relevant to ask whether there are alternative community resources which could improve families' abilities to access cheap necessities. Into this category would come, for instance, bulk-buy purchase of food or nappies or other communal purchase schemes. Sustain, the alliance for better food and farming, in partnership with Oxfam, for example, has helped to develop food projects in many deprived areas of England, including Islington, Rochdale, Barrow-in-Furness, and Coventry. Their approach involves consultations with local communities to identify their particular needs and preferred solutions. These might include providing advice on nutrition and cooking classes in local family and community centres, arranging transport to local supermarkets, and setting up community food-purchasing schemes and cafés (*Guardian*, 2001a).

The rural–urban dimension in relation to family poverty

There has been growing awareness, in recent years, of the difficulties facing rural families and this is particularly important in thinking about community resources in relation to family poverty. However, it is incorrect to suggest that there are two distinct experiences, the 'rural' and the 'urban'. Some families in rural locations will be living in physical isolation and their children may be living a long way from other children. However, in our experience the more typical 'rural' experience is of a family living in a small block or street of social housing on the fringes of more affluent areas, particularly commuter villages. These areas, now increasingly developed and managed by housing associations, have been referred to as 'hidden estates' (by a parent, to one of the authors).

Living on a low income in rural settings is likely to produce a range of difficulties. For example, it may be necessary to travel significant distances to access basic services, such as health care, and to buy reasonably priced food, and there may be problems for children in attending facilities that enhance their social networks, such as youth clubs. These difficulties are illustrated by the following case example from Gill (2001).

> John and Helen Dunmore have three children aged 10, 9 and 3 years. They live in a small village about two and a half miles from the nearest town. The village is an affluent one where the majority of people commute out to work. There is however one street of 'social housing' where the Dunmores live. There are few facilities in the village, particularly for children. There is a weekly youth club but as this is only for children and young people over the age of 11, the Dunmore children are currently excluded. The Dunmores have little contact with their neighbours. They say they are a little wary of the people they live alongside and 'keep themselves to themselves'. One of the problems facing the family is the distance to shops, services, and other amenities. If they need to take one of the children to the doctor they have to walk into town, or else go to the expense of hiring a taxi. Where they live also has implications for their food budget. There is a village shop but the choice is small and the prices are very high. Once a week, John and Helen walk to the supermarket in the town, to do their main shop, and then they have to take a taxi back with the food they have bought.

Financial and benefits advice

As many as 1.5 million households in Britain (7 per cent of all households) lack any financial services, such as a current bank account, home contents insurance or a pension because of a combination of socio-economic circumstances and geographical location (Kempson and Whyley, 1999). It is therefore important to consider whether there are community resources that offer advice about welfare benefits, advocate at a local level for the take-up of benefits, or provide saving facilities. Advice centres, debt advice services, Citizens Advice Bureaux, credit unions, and family centres that offer financial advice will all be important in this respect.

There may also be other services, which are broadly anti-poverty in impact, which are more specific to the needs of the area. For instance, the Community Links *Ground Up* annual (2001) shows a wide range of such community resources being developed across the UK. These include health and nutrition initiatives, such as a microwave loan scheme for families in temporary accommodation, and a food bank that provides a respite food parcel service for families in crisis. They also include income and spending initiatives, such as a children's clothes bank.

Child care resources

Childcare resources in the local community will be very important for parents of younger children. Not only will they be significant at the level of providing new and important experiences for young children but also they will directly impact on other aspects of family life. For instance, through the National Childcare Strategy, there is currently an emphasis on providing childcare places so that lone parents, in particular, can return to work. However, there is a danger that the more favoured and affluent areas are able to access these opportunities more effectively, leading to a widening of the gap between different areas in terms of childcare facilities.

In making an assessment of the availability and value of such local provision for parents, practitioners need to ask questions about its proximity, its flexibility (for instance whether nursery resources are available early in the morning for parents on shift work) and its cost. All of these aspects will have an impact on the value of these resources for individual parents.

In terms of these anti-poverty initiatives and new money for developing services in recent years, there is of course a wide variety of provision in different communities across the UK (see for instance Land, 2002). Again, assessments of community resources and how they impact on the lives of individual families have to be based on thorough local knowledge. These issues are also discussed in Chapter 5 on employment in this volume.

Community resources for children

It is important to look at the experiences of children separately from those of their parents. Parents may, for instance, be actively involved in and supported within their community but their children may be under-resourced in the local community and dependent on only the most basic of statutory provision.

One very important aspect of this will be the very local orientation of children, particularly younger children. For instance, Millward and Wheway (1997) found that 'the outdoor environment within two streets of the front door' was the most significant area, in terms of play for young children. With increased parental anxiety about safety issues, safe play space in close proximity to the family home is likely to continue to be a significant issue (see below).

If parents with low financial resources and at the most demanding stage of the life cycle are necessarily more dependent on their immediate neighbourhood than those in more favoured situations, then children from these families are likely to be particularly exposed to the limitations and difficulties of their neighbourhood. Despite advances in personal transportation and mobility, there is some evidence that, in the last quarter of the twentieth century, children's lives became more constrained. Hillman (1993), for instance, has shown that children's independent mobility has declined. Mobility also varies according to geographical location. In urban areas in the English Midlands, for instance, young people aged 13–14 years have been found to be less likely to travel unaccompanied, even within their home areas, than their peers living in suburban and rural areas, who more commonly travelled alone, even after dark. The young people's decisions about independent travel were based on their perceptions about levels of safety, access, and traffic danger. Most inner-city teenagers in this study felt 'unable to cycle freely, use local parks or travel safely by themselves in their local areas' (Jones, Davis and Eyers, 2000, p326).

Along with this evidence about mobility, there has been an accumulation of information about the pressures that are increasingly experienced by children in the most disadvantaged areas. This has led one group of researchers to conclude that, 'while well designed environments benefit all in society, the impact of negative factors such as cars, vandalism, street gangs and safety are often more apparent for children than for adults. The perceived lack of safety has forced many children back into their homes and away from public space.' (Freeman, Henderson and Kettle, 1999, p116). They go on to argue that 'as children's play range has decreased due largely to growing parental fears for their children's safety, the neighbourhood environment has become increasingly important for play.' (p119). There are clear links here to *social integration*, with these trends leading to a '... loss of social opportunities as fewer people use streets and local facilities so that children have fewer opportunities to observe adults going about their lives outside the home.' (p118).

The perceived safety of local neighbourhoods will also influence the extent to which children are able to access their local community resources, as is illustrated by this case example.

> During consultation, a number of children talked about the fear and uncertainty they experienced because drug takers and pushers lived nearby. One child for instance, said: *'I don't like it when the druggies are around'*.

Services for children

For assessment purposes, services for children can be categorised broadly in the same way as those for their parents, dividing them up into formal, semi-formal and informal categories.

Formal services

The most important formal resources for children will be their schools. Other formal services will include structured work with individual children, mainly on a referral basis, including child and adolescent mental health services, child treatment services provided by social services departments, and the structured child therapy offered by some family centres.

The importance of schools and teachers in child welfare has, until recently, been somewhat neglected by child and family social workers

(Gilligan, 1998), and their employers, to say nothing of government policies and guidance. Amongst all professional groups, teachers are likely to have by far the greatest amount of contact with children. The child's level of achievement, sense of acceptance, and network of peer friendships, including their possible experiences of bullying and unfair discrimination, will all have a profound impact upon their development and future life chances (Sylva, 1994). Research undertaken with children growing up in adverse family and environmental circumstances has shown that one of the most important protective factors associated with resilient children (ie those who thrive, despite many adverse factors in their lives), is a reliable and supportive relationship with an adult outside their immediate family (Werner and Smith, 1992). Whilst this is often likely to be a member of their wider family, it may also be a teacher, or even the parent of a school friend who the child would not otherwise have known. As Gilligan (1998) has noted, schools also play an invaluable role in monitoring the day-to-day well-being of children, as well as offering a potential resource to the whole community.

Whilst educational policies in the UK in recent years have increasingly recognised the central role that educational achievement plays in children's future life chances, we would argue that this has been at the expense of some of the wider social and recreational aspects of education. In this respect, the UK government could learn some important lessons from other European countries, such as Sweden and France, that manage to successfully combine high academic attainment with these social and recreational elements of education, utilising staff with different professional backgrounds working together in the school environment (Moss, Petrie and Poland, 1999).

Given the central importance of schools in children's lives, there are strong incentives for devoting resources towards ensuring that they create inclusive environments for all pupils, and that there are effective services to ensure that children who are experiencing problems are maintained in mainstream provision, wherever possible. Social workers, along with other professionals and agencies working with children and families in local areas, have an important part to play in this aspect of the wider social inclusion agenda (Lloyd, Stead and Kendrick, 2001; Vernon and Sinclair, 1998; Sylva and Evans, 1999). Research in the UK has demonstrated just how effective school-based social work approaches to reducing truancy, school exclusions and delinquency can be, if they are well planned and resourced (Pritchard and Williams, 2001).

Semi-formal services

Semi-formal community resources include activities that are designed to address the specific difficulties or issues that children in the community are facing. They might include groupwork initiatives for children, or activities that are designed with clear criteria for membership and clearly stated outcomes, geared to the needs of particular categories of children.

Examples of such semi-formal community resources would include group resources available for disabled children or for black or dual-heritage children. The following is a case example.

> A family centre on a large primarily white estate became increasingly aware of the difficulties faced by dual-heritage children in the local community. A group was set up for dual-heritage children with the aim of exploring the complexities of their heritage, developing positive identities, and counteracting isolation.

Other examples include mentoring schemes for children with behaviour problems (St James-Roberts and Singh, 2001) and for care leavers (Porteous, 1998), adolescent support teams that aim to divert young people from the care system, typically providing short-term, intensive interventions with the young people and their families (Biehal, Clayden and Byford, 2000), and projects designed to give young people living in more isolated communities better access to services and more involvement in community activities and decision-making (Day, Gilbert and Maitland, 2001).

Informal services

Into the category of informal resources come all of those activities and events within local communities from which children benefit. These might include summer playschemes, youth clubs and other activities with open membership.

Often areas which are disadvantaged do not have a developed social infrastructure of clubs and other activities for children. Also, as we have already pointed out, even where facilities do exist, there may be barriers to certain individuals, or groups of children, making use of them. In assessing the social world of the growing child, it is therefore important to look not just at the provision of these facilities in local communities, but also at the extent to which the child feels she or he can access them.

Black children and children with disabilities may, for instance, perceive that local resources are not open and accessible to them.

Questions about accessibility can also involve transport and levels of family income. As we have already noted, children in poor families are likely to be much more constrained within their local neighbourhood than their better-off peers. The following case example, from a semi-rural setting, illustrates this point.

> Children aged 9–11 in a market town took part in a consultation about facilities in the town. The children lived in the most disadvantaged ward in the centre of the town, which scored highest on the indices of deprivation including child poverty (DTER, 2000). The town's main facilities, including the sports centre, were in the south of the town. Analysing the results of the consultation, it was clear that the children were not saying that the town did not have facilities, but some felt that they did not have access to these facilities because of the cost and the difficulty of transport. As one 10-year-old said, *'living here you need a parent with a car'*.

An example of the long-term benefits that children can derive from informal community-based resources is provided by the work of Holman and colleagues on two adjoining estates in Bath (Holman, 1981; 2000). The project, set up in the 1970s, consisted of open-access youth clubs for youngsters of different age groups, run continuously over a number of years, offering trips, holidays and activities for all who attended, as well as individual support for young people with personal difficulties. Using a range of measures of vulnerability, including low family income, poor child-rearing, educational difficulties, large family size, and disrupted/lone-parent family, Holman estimated that 70 per cent of a study group of 51 youngsters, followed-up between 12 and 23 years later, had been at 'high' or 'medium' risk for adverse development, particularly future offending.

Holman found that only a quarter of the children in the study group were judged to have displayed either 'very unsatisfactory behaviour' (4 per cent), or to have given some 'cause for concern' (22 per cent), when aged 16–19 years. In adulthood, only one person (2 per cent) was considered to be living a 'very unsatisfactory life' and a further six people (12 per cent) were judged to be leading 'unsatisfactory' lives, leaving well over eight out of every ten members of the study group who were judged to be leading 'satisfactory' lives. While this is a small sample of all of the young people involved in this project and, as Holman acknowledges, the project cannot necessarily claim to have been the most important factor in these young people's lives, nonetheless these are encouraging outcomes for such a group of vulnerable young people. Certainly, a large proportion of those interviewed for the retrospective study (Holman, 2000) claimed that their involvement in these activities positively influenced their development and played a significant role in countering the disadvantages that they experienced in their childhoods.

A number of factors were identified as significant in the success of the approach developed in this project. Among the most important were: the style of leadership, characterised as friendly, approachable, trustworthy, and well organised; the support of the local community; and a long-term commitment from leaders who lived in the local area. As already indicated, the fact that the clubs were open to all young people in the area avoided stigmatising those who chose to attend, and provided an environment in which the more vulnerable children could integrate and make friends with peers who were living in more favourable home circumstances and performing better within school.

Unfortunately, as Holman himself acknowledges(2000, pp96–103), these successful ingredients of his project are not fashionable in today's political climate of short-term, targeted interventions, working to nationally set performance criteria. It is evidence like this that might be important for workers to use when they are arguing for the longer-term engagement of children and parents with resources in their local areas.

Access to play

As already stated, access to appropriate local play facilities is a very important aspect of the experience of all children as they are developing. There are a number of elements involved in the assessment of the play facilities available to children in different settings.

The first is whether there is good-quality play equipment located in the immediate vicinity. In many local neighbourhoods the play facilities are either very limited or in a very poor state of repair. The second element is the safety of the equipment provided and, if the child is to go on his or her own, the safety of their route to the play area. There is much practice evidence of children being unable to access local play facilities because of dangerous roads, or the threat posed by the presence of dangerous individuals, or groups of older children congregating in play areas.

Once again, it is the children who live in the most deprived circumstances who are often at greatest risk. There is a clear association between lower socio-economic status and higher rates of deaths and serious injuries in accidents, both on the roads and in the home (Spencer, 1996).

One clear reason for this is that the most disadvantaged children often live in the most dense housing areas with the highest rates of traffic flow. Despite repeated public education programmes, designed to change individual behaviour in relation to such issues as 'road safety', the research evidence is clear that changes to the physical environment are much more effective in reducing road accidents among children (Stone, 1993).

One interesting example of such a change, imported from continental Europe, is the current trialing of 'home zones' by certain local authorities, with some financial support from central government (*Guardian*, 1999; 2001b). Home zones consist of one or more residential streets where very low speed limits for vehicles are combined with traffic-calming measures and the introduction of trees, seating and other environmental changes, designed to give pedestrians clear priority over cars and to create safe play areas for children in localities that are not well provided with alternative play areas. Not only are such home zones known to reduce child deaths and injuries on the roads – the principal cause of death in children under 15 years of age – but they can also help to create a greater sense of community and security for all local residents, who are also involved in the planning and design of such schemes.

Home zones represent only a small part of the government's wider community regeneration agenda, which includes the National Strategy for Neighbourhood Renewal, the New Deal for Communities, and strategic use of the Single Regeneration Budget, alongside a whole host of other initiatives targeted at different groups, such as Sure Start for parents of pre-school children, and the Children's Fund for children aged 5–13 years. Whilst the political attention and extra funding that these social inclusion initiatives are currently receiving is to be welcomed, the shortcomings of current approaches have also been noted by various academic researchers and social policy analysts (Shaw et al, 1999). In particular, the sheer complexity of the current policy landscape, and the rejection of universal approaches in favour of targeting funding only towards the most deprived areas of concentrated need, mean that many millions of households, often living in very deprived circumstances, are currently being denied any additional resources at all under these measures.

Anti-poverty resources for children

All of the above community resources can be seen to be broadly 'anti-poverty' initiatives in the sense that they are located in the poorest areas. However, a number of more direct anti-poverty resources can be provided for children in local areas.

There may, for instance, be breakfast clubs which research has shown have benefits, not only in terms of nutrition, but also in terms of their social impact. Breakfast clubs may also provide out-of-school care for children at the start of the day, thereby supporting parents who are going out to work.

In addition, there may be local facilities and community resources that can include children in activities that they would otherwise not be able to experience, because of their family's low income, such as local schemes that organise outings or holidays.

The family's use of community resources

It is central to the ecological perspective that the interaction between the family and the available community resources should be assessed. Whilst a particular community may be relatively well provided with resources for families, some families may be largely uninvolved and therefore not benefit. Many factors can affect a family's use of community resources. These include the family's level of knowledge of the existence of resources, their understanding of the potential benefits of these resources, and their confidence in accessing them.

At a wider level, much will depend on the family's sense of belonging and involvement in the community. It is a common practice experience, for instance, to work with families who do not identify with their community and who perceive their future to involve moving away from where they are currently living. Once there is this level of disassociation from the community, then the use of community resources becomes more unlikely and uncertain.

Equally important will be the family's perception of how its members are regarded by the community. If a family feels ostracised, with a resulting sense of isolation, then they are unlikely to feel able to access the resources that the community has to offer. Again, it is a common practice experience that families feel unable to access community resources because they perceive that they will not be accepted.

Issues for assessment

The assessment of community resources necessitates adopting a wider perspective on the analysis of the welfare of children and families. It challenges workers and organisations to look at not only the internal dynamics of the family but also how these internal dynamics interact with external community resources. For instance, with the availability of adequate external resources the parent who is experiencing childcare pressures may be able to survive. Without such resources the pressures may be overwhelming.

Effective external resources will not only be those which directly address difficulties within the family or provide practical and financial support. They will also be all of those resources in the community which bring contact with other parents and neighbours and in so doing enhance natural networks for both children and parents.

Recognising the importance of community resources in terms of children's development and parents' ability to cope with the demands of childcare necessitates changes on the part of workers and the agencies that employ them. It requires that workers become more familiar with both formal and informal resources within local communities. To understand the family's access or potential access to community resources workers must have an up-to-date picture of what is available within local communities. This in turn necessitates new partnerships being developed with the providers of resources in the local community. Social workers need not only to recognise the importance of such community resources but also to foster their strengths.

It is also important to develop new ways of listening to and understanding children and parents when they talk about what resources they have access to and how these resources impact on their lives. This exploration will involve understanding the ease with which people can access resources in the community – not only in terms of physical access but also in terms of the information that local community resources provide and in terms of the perceptions of children and parents of these resources. Do parents and children know what is provided? Do they know how to make contact? Are the resources regarded as 'cliquey'?

Are they regarded as stigmatising? Do the parents and children have the personal skills and confidence to access them?

From an ecological perspective it is also crucial to understand the interconnections between community resources and the other assessment categories on the 'missing' side of the triangle.

For instance it will be important to ask how community resources facilitate *social integration* and at the same time how their effective use may be determined by the degree of social integration. Also *income* and *employment* will be important in terms of the family's ability to access resources. Many resources will be closed to people on low incomes. Children's leisure activities, which have become increasingly commercialised, may be particularly inaccessible to poor children. Housing and its location will also be important in terms of the family's ability to access resources.

References

Aldgate, J and Statham, J (2001) *The Children Act Now: Messages from research.* London: The Stationery Office

Audit Commission (1994) *Seen But not Heard.* London: HMSO

Barn, R, Sinclair, R, Ferdinand, D (1997) *Acting on Principle: An examination of race and ethnicity in Social Services provision for children and families.* London: BAAF

Beresford, B, Sloper, P, Baldwin, S, Newman, T (1996) *What Works in Services for Families with a Disabled Child?* Barkingside: Barnardo's

Biehal, N, Clayden J, Byford, S (2000) *Home or Away? Supporting young people and families.* London: National Children's Bureau

Burrows, R (1997) *Contemporary Patterns of Residential Mobility in Relation to Social Housing in England.* York: University of York

Community Links (2001) *Ground Up.* London

Davis, J and Ridge, T (1997) *Same Scenery, Different Lifestyle: Rural children on a low income.* London: The Children's Society

Day, E, Gilbert, D, Maitland, L (2001) *Empowering young people in rural Suffolk: an evaluation report for the Home Office* (no. 234). London: Home Office

DETR (2000) *Indices of Deprivation.* London: DETR

Department of Transport (2002) Statistical Release TR-013 13 June 2002

Freeman, C, Henderson, P, Kettle, J (1999) *Planning with Children for Better Communities.* Bristol: The Policy Press

Garbarino, J and Crouter, A (1978) Defining the community context of parent-child relations; the correlates of child mistreatment. *Child Development*, **49**, 604–16

Ghate, D, Shaw, C, Hazel, N (2000) *Fathers and Family Centres: Engaging fathers in preventive services*. York: York Publishing Services

Gill, O (2001) *Invisible Children: Child and family poverty in Bristol, Bath, Gloucestershire, Somerset and Wiltshire*. Barkingside: Barnardo's

Gilligan, R (1998) The importance of schools and teachers in child welfare, *Child and Family Social Work*, **3**, 13–25

Gilroy, P (1987) *There Ain't No Black in the Union Jack*. London: Hutchinson

Gordon, D, Parker, R, Loughron, F (2000) *Disabled Children in Britain. A re-analysis of the OPCS disability survey*. London: The Stationery Office

Grimshaw, R and McGuire, C (1998) *Evaluating Parenting Programmes: A study of stakeholders' views*. London: National Children's Bureau

Guardian (1999) Street Lives, 3 March (Society, pp6–7)

Guardian (2001a) Diet Pep Talks, 25 July (Society, p5)

Guardian (2001b) Streets Ahead, 1 August (Society, p4)

Hillman, M (1993) One false move: A study of children's independent mobility.' In M Hillman (ed) *Children, Transport and the Quality of Life*. London: Policy Studies Institute

Holman, R (1981) *Kids at the Door*. Oxford: Blackwell

Holman, R (2000) *Kids at the Door Revisited*. Lyme Regis: Russell House Publishing

Jones, L, Davis, A, Eyers, T (2000) Young people, transport and risk: comparing access and independent mobility in urban, suburban and rural environments. *Health Education Journal*, **59**, 315–28

Kempson, E and Whyley, C (1999) *Kept Out or Opted Out? Understanding and combating financial exclusion*. Partridge Green, West Sussex: Policy Press

Land, H (2002) *Meeting the Child Poverty Challenge*. London: The Daycare Trust

Lloyd, E (1999) *What Works in Parenting Education?* Barkingside: Barnardo's

Lloyd, G, Stead, J, Kendrick, A (2001) *'Hanging On In There': A study of inter-agency work to prevent school exclusion in three local authorities*, London: National Children's Bureau

Macdonald, G and Roberts, H (1995) *What Works in the Early Years?* Barkingside: Barnardo's

Macdonald, G with Winkley, A (1999) *What Works in Child Protection?* Barkingside: Barnardo's

Millward, A and Wheway, R (1997) Facilitating play on housing estates. *Findings*, no 217, York: Joseph Rowntree Foundation

Moss, P, Petrie, P, Poland, G (1999) *Rethinking School: Some international perspectives*. Leicester: National Youth Agency

Porteous, D (1998) *Evaluation of the CSV On-Line Mentoring Scheme*. London: Community Service Volunteers

Pritchard, C and Williams, R (2001) A three-year comparative longitudinal study of a school-based social work family service to reduce truancy. *Journal of Social Welfare and Family Law*, **23** (1), 23–43

Qureshi, T, Berridge, D, Wenman, H (2000) *Family Support for South Asian Communities: A case study*. London: National Children's Bureau

Roberts, H (2000) *What Works in Reducing Inequalities in Child Health?* Barkingside: Barnardo's

Sharma, N (2002) *Still Missing Out?; Ending poverty and social exclusion: messages to government from families with disabled children*. Barkingside: Barnardo's

Shaw, M, Dorling, D, Gordon, D, Davey-Smith, G (1999) *The Widening Gap: Health inequalities and policy in Britain*. Bristol: The Policy Press

Singh, J (1992) *Black Families and Respite Care*. Barkingside: Barnardo's

Smith, C and Pugh, G (1996) *Learning to be a Parent: A survey of group-based parenting programmes*. London: Family Policy Studies Centre

Spencer, N (1996) Reducing child health inequalities. In P Bywaters and E McLeod (eds) *Working for Equality in Health*, pp143–60. London: Routledge

St James-Roberts, I and Singh, CS (2001) *Can Mentors Help Primary School Children with Behaviour Problems?* (Home Office Research Study No. 233). London: Home Office

Statham, J (2000) *Outcomes and Effectiveness of Family Support Services: A research review*. London: Institute of Education, University of London

Stone, D (1993) *Costs and Benefits of Accident Prevention: A selective review of the literature*. Glasgow: Public Health Research Unit, University of Glasgow

Sylva, K (1994) School influences on children's development. *Journal of Child Psychology and Psychiatry*, **35**, 135–72

Sylva, K and Evans, E (1999) Preventing failure at school. *Children and Society*, **13**, 278–86

Thoburn, J, Wilding, J, Watson, J (2000) *Family Support in Cases of Emotional Maltreatment and Neglect*. London: The Stationery Office

Vernon, J and Sinclair, R (1998) *Maintaining Children in School: The contribution of social services department*, London: National Children's Bureau

Werner, E and Smith, R (1992) *Overcoming the Odds: High-risk children from birth to adulthood*. Ithaca: Cornell University Press

Williams, F (1993) Women and community. In J Bornat, C Periera, D Pilgrim, F Williams (eds) *Community Care: A reader*, pp33–42. Basingstoke: Macmillan

Social integration 3

In the guidelines accompanying the Assessment Framework, social integration is defined as:

'(an) exploration of the wider context of the local neighbourhood and community and its impact on the child and parents. (It) includes the degree of the family's integration or isolation, their peer groups, friendships and social networks and the importance attached to them.' (Department of Health, 2000, p23)

Family's social integration

Obviously there are clear links with the other assessment categories on the bottom side of the triangle. Social integration, for instance, will have an impact on *employment* and work opportunities, as demonstrated in a study of young people living in two rural locations in Scotland (Pavis, Platt and Hubbard, 2000). Informal networks of personal relationships were found to be of central importance to securing both employment and accommodation, and a 'bad' reputation, related to personal difficulties, in these relatively tight-knit communities, made securing work almost impossible.

The degree of social integration will also have an impact on the family's likelihood of accessing *community resources*. For instance, although there may be resources within a local community, if there is a low degree of social integration, vulnerable families may have neither the knowledge nor the opportunities to access them. There will also be strong connections between the extent of social integration and the characteristics of the *wider family* networks. A large number of UK community studies since the 1960s have pointed to the complexity of these connections. In spite of high degrees of social mobility, neighbourhood and family network patterns often continue to be interwoven at a very local level.

Specific evidence of the links between social integration and a range of other factors is provided by numerous research studies conducted in different countries around the world. For example, researchers in Chicago have examined the links between juvenile crime and neighbourhood social integration (Sampson, Morenoff and Earls, 1999). They utilise (and extend) the concept of social capital, which consists of the trust, co-operation, reciprocity, and community identity generated by the everyday interactions between individuals within their social networks (Coleman, 1988; Puttnam, 1993). From this, they developed their own concept, called 'collective efficacy', to describe how the potential benefits of social capital can be transformed into effective action to prevent juvenile offending in 'high-risk' areas. They found that, in similarly deprived inner-city areas, rates of violent crime were lower in areas with higher collective efficacy, where mutual trust among neighbours was combined with a willingness to intervene in order to maintain public order. In areas scoring high on collective efficacy, crime rates were as much as 40 per cent lower than in otherwise similar neighbourhoods with lower collective efficacy. In this way, they demonstrated that crime is not simply a function of the demographic or socio-economic circumstances of an area, but that it is also dependent on the neighbourhood's social integration. Levels of collective efficacy were improved by residential stability and undermined by poverty and proximity to other areas of concentrated poverty. Similar findings emerge in relation to area variations in rates of child abuse and neglect, as we go on to consider later in this chapter.

There is also a large volume of research evidence that examines the various ways in which the social networks of both adults and children are linked to their individual circumstances and characteristics, including their geographical location, age, gender, socio-economic position, level of education, marital status, and various personality traits (Jack, 2000). Fischer (1982), for example, found that adults living in rural areas of the United States tended to have more dense and kin-based networks of relationships, compared to those in urban areas, who displayed more widely dispersed networks of relationships that included more friends. Higher levels of education and income also tend to be associated with larger, more widely dispersed networks, consisting of more intimate relationships (Werner, 1995). It is also accepted that, in general, women tend to enjoy more stable, confiding relationships than men, but that these differences are also influenced by marital status, with single mothers, for example, tending to rely on smaller networks than otherwise similar mothers in two-parent families (Jack, 2000). Overall, the social networks developed and maintained by individual parents and children tend to reflect their general position in the society in which they live. As Jack notes: 'Often, the groups or individuals who are in the greatest need of additional, more reliable, or more satisfying sources of social support, are those who are least likely to have access to these things.' (Jack, 2000, p714)

Throughout this volume we emphasise the importance of examining the experience of the child as well as that of the parent in the family. There will be many complex connections between the child's social integration into his or her community and neighbourhood and the parents' social integration. But there may well be significant differences as well and it is important to examine these differences and to focus equally on the child's experience of her or his social world, as on that of the parents. Parental social integration is not necessarily an indication of children's integration. The child's social integration may be problematic and fragmented, even when the parent is socially well integrated, and vice versa.

The definition used in relation to social integration in the guidelines refers to community. Again the connotations around the word may not reflect the real experience of parents and children, which may be characterised by deep-seated divisions and conflicts based on such factors as age, social class, race, gender, disability and sexuality. Differences of identity and power structure people's experiences of community and neighbourhood, and may lead to social exclusion, rather than integration for certain groups and individuals (Williams, 1993; Gilroy, 1987). In reality, therefore, 'community' and the social interactions surrounding vulnerable families, may be negative, rather than positive, in their impact. The family that does not fit in may be ostracised. More directly, children's experience may be very damaging and negative in relation to the people they are living alongside. Also, the perceptions of community and neighbourhood may be very different for children and parents. Children, for instance, may have a much more local and immediate conception of community and neighbourhood.

UK research on links between area of residence and child welfare

A small body of UK research links rates of child mistreatment (usually excluding sexual abuse) to neighbourhood and area of residence. For instance, Cotterill (1988) analysed child abuse rates for an inner London borough and found that 50 per cent of the child abuse registrations occurred in what he discovered to be 'eight persistent target areas'. He suggested that this concentration of child abuse cases could not be explained solely by levels of social disadvantage, and that other factors were important in terms of why particular neighbourhoods were linked to high rates of child abuse. A decade later Baldwin and Carruthers (1998), in work carried out in Coventry, made a detailed map of child protection referrals in the area. Like Cotterill, they reported a distinct clustering of child protection cases in particular areas.

Other UK research has suggested the importance of neighbourhood networks for parents. Jean Packman and her colleagues, in their study of the reception of children into state care, showed that only a small number of parents had looked to friends and neighbours for support (Packman, Randall and Jacques, 1986). They also showed that parents attached higher importance to neighbourhood and area of residence than social workers.

The importance of locality to families is also underlined by other UK research, including a study by Gibbons (1990) of family support and prevention in different local areas, which concluded that 'availability of people to give practical help with money, childcare and other domestic tasks appeared important in reducing personal stress caused by high levels of family problems.' (p117). Another study of family support (Gardner, 1992) concluded that, among the interventions which were considered most helpful, by both the workers and the parents, were those that supported social networks.

Finally, a study of an area of Bristol which had high child protection rates and child welfare concerns (Gill et al, 2000), showed the significance of the complex intertwining of family and neighbourhood networks. Some of the most vulnerable families had very limited network supports at a local level. This study drew attention to the high mobility experienced by some of the more vulnerable families, which in turn was likely to impact on their networks of support.

US research on isolation, networks and social support

Research carried out in other parts of the world, particularly the United States, offers a more detailed exploration of the significance of network support in relation to child welfare. This work is rich in its suggestions of the importance of the relationship between the internal and external worlds of the family. However it is important to recognise the different cultural contexts in which this research has been carried out and to be wary of automatically transferring such research findings to the situation in the UK. Not only are the processes that structure the communities and neighbourhoods of the US and other countries different (for instance the workings of the housing market), but also the traditions of community institutions and organisations are different. Even more important, however, is the differences between countries in the cultural context of community and neighbourhood. Many of the studies in this body of literature have also been carried out with specific groups of children and parents, particularly in terms of racial background.

Nonetheless, in the absence of comparable UK research, the US and other international research can give powerful pointers to the significance of the relationship between community and neighbourhood and what happens within families.

In the US there is a strand of research, going back more than two decades, that examines the significance of isolation and lack of support in relation to parents' ability to perform their role effectively. Much of this work was completed in the 1980s. Reviewing this work, Maluccio (1989, p273) concluded that '... on the basis of evidence from research studies and demonstration projects, it is reasonable to conclude that social supports can play a preventative as well as ameliorative function with vulnerable families and children especially moderating stress and producing buffering effects on well-being.' During that period there was also evidence about the significance of parents' networks of support for even small babies. For instance Tracey and Whittaker (1987) showed that mothers with greater social support tend to demonstrate more sensitive responses to their infants.

More specifically, the last two decades have seen an exploration of the links between lack of support for parents and child mistreatment. We will not give an exhaustive overview of this work, but rather will refer to pieces of research that are representative of this body of work. However, Thompson (1995) gives an excellent review of this work, up until the mid-1990s.

Starr (1982) looked at a wide range of family and individual characteristics to ascertain the links between these characteristics and an increased statistical likelihood of child mistreatment. Using two groups, one which was comprised of parents who had been identified as abusing their children and a control group in which abuse had not been recorded, Starr concluded that social isolation was one of the few significant characteristics to distinguish the two groups. However, in this early work, the complexity of the concepts of social support and social isolation was already becoming apparent. Belle (1982) indicated the complex two-way nature of giving and receiving social support. She found that maintaining social ties may, in itself, be a cause of considerable stress for low-income families. Belle's work illustrates the important point that social contact cannot always be assumed to be beneficial and may in itself be a cause of stress.

Crittenden (1985) again confirmed the importance of social networks for parenting, although she found no clear statistical association with child mistreatment. She did, however, show an association between maternal patterns of social support and the child's security of attachment. Another study (Crnic et al, 1984) found that mothers' stress and social support were significant predictors of maternal attitudes and the quality of interaction with their infants, over an 18-month period. This study did, however, find that the longer-term predictability of the association was poor.

Throughout this period, the general importance of social isolation for parenting was being confirmed by a number of US studies. Polansky and his colleagues, for instance, found that women who they referred to as 'neglectful mothers' reported that less support was available from their informal networks than was reported for a control group (Polansky et al, 1985). These mothers also perceived the neighbourhoods in which they lived as being less friendly than did a control group, who lived in the same areas. Moncher (1995) extended the analysis of the relationship between social isolation and child mistreatment by showing that social isolation and lack of social support may be linked to particular types of child mistreatment. His results indicated that certain aspects of support – concrete support from work or school associates and emotional support in non-critical relationships – were important in predicting decreased potential for physical child abuse to occur.

However, Coohey (1996) stressed the difficulty of determining what constitutes social isolation. Her study showed that 'neglectful mothers' had more limited networks with fewer members. But she argued that these networks could not be characterised as social isolation. It is not only the extent of networks that is important but also their quality.

International research on neighbourhood and child mistreatment

Over the last two decades another body of research has been developed in the US and elsewhere that is relevant to our consideration of social integration. This starts at the level of community, rather than the individual family, and sets out to relate various community characteristics to different rates of child mistreatment within those communities. This work has aimed to distinguish, at a community level, the characteristics that may be associated with child mistreatment, but gives valuable pointers for understanding the nature and degree of the social integration of the family.

This research has drawn on other traditions within sociological enquiring, most notably the study of crime and delinquency. In both the US and the UK there has been a long tradition of linking delinquent behaviour to neighbourhood culture, normative controls at a neighbourhood level and levels of social disorganisation (see, for instance, Sampson, Morenoff and Earls, 1999; Simcha-Fagan and Schwarz, 1986).

More than two decades ago Garbarino and Crouter (1978) showed that a combination of socio-economic disadvantage, maternal stress and high geographic mobility might be associated with increased levels of child mistreatment. In research that developed this theme, Garbarino and Sherman (1980) compared two neighbourhoods which were matched on socio-economic factors but had different rates of child mistreatment. The mothers interviewed in the areas with higher levels of child abuse did not necessarily see themselves as lacking potential support. However, they did see themselves as performing their role as parents in a situation in which there were lower levels of reciprocity and less asking of help from neighbours.

An Australian study (Vinson, Baldry and Hargreaves, 1996) followed the earlier work of Garbarino and his colleagues in studying two adjacent areas that were matched in terms of socio-economic characteristics but had different levels of reported child mistreatment. Vinson and his colleagues found a significant difference in the structure of the social networks that characterised families in the two areas. In the area with a higher rate of child mistreatment, there was a relative lack of connection between the immediate and the more distant parts of the families' social networks. The researchers hypothesised that the association between this difference in network connections and the differing rates of child mistreatment might lie in a number of factors. In the higher child mistreatment area, with more limited connections between the immediate and more distant parts of the network, there could be less scope for (beneficial) influences on child-rearing practices. Secondly, there would be less cultural influence on how parents should cope with difficulty and stress. And finally there was likely to be less monitoring of child rearing by the wider community.

Another important aspect of the characteristics of neighbourhoods and the social networks within them is the extent of mobility into and out of the area. In the US literature the 'social disorganisation' associated with high mobility has been found to be linked to a range of problems, including juvenile delinquency and child mistreatment. On the basis of the research overview conducted by Thompson, referred to above (Thompson, 1995), possible links between high rates of social disorganisation and child mistreatment can be attributed to:

- the disengagement of the family from the community
- less sharing of resources
- little awareness of local services.
- limited social capital
- children's more limited social networks.

Practice experience in relation to family's social integration

A great deal of practice experience also points to the significance of neighbourhood and community factors for parenting capacity and child development. It is our experience that, when parents talk about the challenges of bringing up children, the difficulties that they face within the confines of their families are often linked with what is going on outside their families, particularly at a neighbourhood level.

Disadvantages in *income*, *housing*, and *employment* will often be compounded by and directly associated with relationship difficulties at a neighbourhood level. People who have little power in relation to these factors will, through the mechanisms of the housing market and social housing allocations, often be housed in the most disadvantaged areas. This is not necessarily a conscious process on the part of housing authorities, but its impact is nevertheless very significant.

Parents with dependent children who live in disadvantaged areas and on low incomes are likely to be particularly affected by the characteristics of their neighbourhood. There are two reasons for this. Firstly, they are likely to have fewer resources to travel outside the neighbourhood for social contact, entertainment, or purchasing food and family necessities. Secondly, they will be constrained by their stage in the life cycle. Having young children will constrain them and in many ways lock them into the local neighbourhood. This constraint into and by the neighbourhood, for the most disadvantaged families, has a number of important implications for assessment. It is important to be aware of the significance this may have in parents' lives and the different aspects of neighbourhood, which will impact on parents.

Practice experience shows that parents often talk about a number of interconnected aspects of the neighbourhood which have implications for social integration. These include neighbours and safety, for example. Being significantly constrained by where they live, parents will be particularly affected by their near neighbours. The following practice example illustrates this.

> Bob and Kirsty are parents in their late 20s who have two young children. In the past there had been significant childcare difficulties. They have recently been moved to a block of flats on a large peripheral estate. Next door, across the stairwell, is another young couple but without children. There is constant noise coming from the flat and people calling at all times of the day and night. Bob and Kirsty talk a great deal about how the situation has a very bad effect on them and their children.

Parents are likely to be particularly alive to the threats of their neighbourhood, to both themselves and their children. Dangerous roads, for instance, immediately next to residential streets and blocks of flats, can have an impact on the social integration of the area. Parents may feel cut off and surrounded by a dangerous environment. Equally, the perception that there are dangerous people in the area can have an impact on social integration. The high level of drug dealing, for example, in many deprived areas can have a major impact on personal safety and sense of security, thereby limiting social integration in an area. For instance one of the parents interviewed by Gill and his colleagues (Gill et al, 2000) illustrated the fear of encroaching danger experienced by many parents:

> 'The drug dealers are beginning to get closer too. They are nearer our homes now. They used to be all around the outside but now they are on your own street.'

At a more general level, parents talk about the extent to which they get support as well as experience stress, as a result of the people they live alongside. Again, a case example serves to illustrate these influences of local relationships.

> Jane Edmunds is a lone parent with two children, Michael aged 9 and Sophie aged 6. Jane struggles to bring up her children well. She talks a lot about the support and pressures she experiences in her neighbourhood. These descriptions become interwoven with her descriptions of the difficulties she is facing with her children. She talks about good neighbours who will 'look out' for her. But she also talks about the fear and stress of children knocking at her door, breaking her windows and verbally abusing her.

Children's social integration

An increasing range of research focuses on the social integration of children. For example, educational research related to peer group relations, and sociological studies of crime and delinquency are both relevant to this area of enquiry. As in previous sections we can only refer to some of the main themes of this work which produce pointers for the understanding of the social integration of children

In considering children's social integration it is important to recognise the connections and links, not only with the other categories on this side of the triangle, but also with the other two sides, focusing on child development and parenting capacity. For example, the number of adults and children in a child's social network has been found to be associated with the child's performance on IQ tests. Feiring and Lewis (1989) found this association remained statistically significant even when children were matched in terms of socio-economic circumstances. These interactions go to the heart of the ecological perspective on child and family assessment.

In relation to the interaction between the child's social integration and the other domains on the bottom side of the triangle, recent research in the UK has shown that, for example, there are important connections between the family's income position and the nature of children's social involvement outside the home (see, for instance, Ridge, 2002).

In earlier work Ridge and Davis (1997) gave a case example which illustrated the connections between income, housing and social integration in a rural context. This case example clearly shows the connections that are central to an ecological perspective on the welfare of children.

> Allison and Linda live in a small village on a low income. They attend a secondary school in a large town some distance from their home. They are unable to see friends after school because their mother cannot afford the petrol to take them. Allison is aware of what her friends are doing together after school and feels very left out of things, especially when they are talking over what they did together the night before. Her family's house is already cramped and overcrowded and having friends to stay the night is not an option.

More generally, there will be connections between the area of residence and the kind of *housing* provision that is available to the family, on the one hand, and the nature and degree of *social integration* experienced by the child, on the other. The type of housing and the social demographic mix of the neighbourhood will both play a part in shaping the child's experience of relationships and the degree of social integration that the child experiences. And finally there will be connections between the child's social integration and the nature and extent of the *community resources* that are available. Accessible play areas and the existence of clubs, for example, can play important parts in shaping the child's social interactions.

Other important neighbourhood factors may also be at work in shaping the child's social integration. One of the most significant of these will be the safety of the local neighbourhood environment. If the locality is safe for children then this can have an effect in promoting social integration. If, on the other hand, the local neighbourhood is dangerous then it will impact negatively on the child's social integration.

Some neighbourhood and community settings will be damaging for children's sense of self-worth and well-being. Children can find their environment alien and hostile as a result, for instance, of living in large blocks of flats or damaged housing areas. Such experiences will lend little support to the child's sense of self-worth, and this in turn is likely to have an impact on their social integration.

In all of this, it is important to recognise that the child's own perceptions of his or her networks and degree of social integration is likely to be the significant factor, rather than an 'objective' analysis of these factors. Research with 5–14-year-olds demonstrates children's ability to differentiate between the sort of relationships that they have with different members of their social networks. Not surprisingly, most children in this age group perceive their mothers to be the best general providers of all types of social support, whilst friends are viewed as the best source of companionship, and teachers receive high scores for the provision of information, as do fathers (Reid et al, 1989). These findings have obvious implications, not only for the content of the assessments that are eventually produced, but also for the process by which these are obtained.

Age of child and social integration

From a very early age, a child will be affected by the wider social world that surrounds the family into which they are born. The level of social contacts that the parent has and the richness of their social world can have direct implications for the child's development from a very young age. If the parents' networks are developed and extended, through their involvement with community-based projects, enabling the child to come into contact with a richer diversity of network members, this can have implications for the child's development from a very young age. At the current time, in the UK, this may be one of the benefits of the community and group-based approaches of some of the new Sure Start and Children's Fund initiatives. In developing group initiatives and activities for the parents of young children, the richness of the children's social world is enhanced and the increased stimulation and variety is beneficial for the child's development.

As the child grows the significance of relationships outside the home increases, and different aspects of the relationships, such as intimacy, self-disclosure and emotional support grow in importance. Gender differences begin to emerge by middle childhood, with girls tending to develop more intimate friendships than boys. There is an increasing association between the quality of friendships, for both boys and girls, and their general levels of adjustment and emotional difficulties (Dunn, 1993). During adolescence, most young people begin to rely less on their parents and start to invest more in their relationships with their peers. In absolute terms, parental relationships are still of central importance but they are likely to be characterised by increasing levels of conflict, as well as continuing levels of support in most cases (Dunn and McGuire, 1992).

However, besides noting general trends, which hold true for the majority of children, it is also important to be aware of different patterns of social relationships for different groups of children. Particularly important may be variations in social relationships for children who belong to different ethnic groups, or who live in different family structures. Cochran and Riley (1990), for instance, found significant differences according to ethnicity and family structure for groups of 6-year-old children living in the USA. They found different patterns of relationships for black and white children, in both one-parent and two-parent families. They put these findings into a neighbourhood and class context, suggesting that low income parents, many of whom were African-Americans, were actively discouraging social contacts between their children and some of their neighbours, if they were perceived to be different and potentially dangerous.

The crucial point for workers undertaking assessments is that they should examine levels of social integration within the context of the expectations and norms of different groups, rather than from an assumed view of what constitutes 'normal' relations for the child outside the family environment.

Links between peer relationships and behavioural difficulties

There is another informative strand of research in the US which looks at the links between children's and young people's peer relationships and behaviour difficulties.

Buysse (1977), for example, looked at the relationship between the characteristics of adolescents' social networks, personal resources and environmental risks and the extent and type of behaviour problems that they exhibited. He concluded that perceived conflicts in social networks were associated with behaviour problems. He did, however, also conclude that environmental risk factors impacted on the type of behaviour problem. In this body of research, therefore, although the focus is on peer relationships, there is again an emphasis on the impact of other factors and the wider ecology of children's and young people's lives.

Some years later Stocker (1994) studied the connections between children's psychological adjustment and individual differences in their perceptions of relationships with siblings, mothers and friends. Her results indicated that there was a correlation between the children's loneliness, depressive mood, self-esteem, and behaviour, and the characteristics of their social relationships. She argued that as well as relationships affecting adjustment, it is also possible that adjustment influences the quality of children's relationships. She suggested, for instance, that children with high self-esteem are likely to be more confident in developing relationships.

In assessing children's relationships outside the family, it is necessary to be alive to the complexity of social networks. One aspect that has been emphasised is that some children who are viewed negatively by their peer group may nevertheless report that they have close friends – often children like themselves who are socially rejected by the majority. Hartup (1996), for instance, distinguishes between acceptance or rejection by the wider peer group and friendships between two children, which may affect their development in either positive or negative ways.

Deater-Deckard (2001) has provided an overview of research into the links between peer relationships and the development of psychopathology. The review looks at the relationship between rejection by peers and both internalised and externalised behaviour problems. It showed that children with externalising behaviour problems found it difficult to gain acceptance by their peers and these behaviour problems were maintained as a result of this rejection. Children who were aggressive or hyperactive were much more likely to be avoided or ostracised by their peers, because larger groups tended to isolate those individuals who disrupted normal peer interactions. In relation to the internalisation of problems, the evidence suggests that patterns of withdrawal from social interaction are consistent over time and in different contexts, and that there is a relationship between withdrawal in childhood relationships and subsequent levels of depression in adult life.

One complexity of the research in this area is that children differ in their sensitivity to rejection by their peers. It is the children who are highest in this 'rejection sensitivity' who show the most aggression and problems in peer relationships. In addition, Deater-Deckard refers to work by Bulkley (2000) that suggests that there may be considerable differences in the significance attached to rejection by different groups of adolescents, and that these attitudes may differ across ethnic groups.

The most extreme form of rejection is, of course, bullying. There are increasing indications that this form of victimisation may be experienced by even very young (pre-school) children. Again, the experience of this extreme form of rejection is likely to be linked to internalised difficulties, such as depression.

Links between children's relationships, social networks, and child mistreatment

Research has also been carried out, again primarily in the US, which looks at the connection between children's social networks, and child mistreatment.

This body of research does not, however, point to unidirectional links, of a linear nature. It does not indicate, for instance, that the mistreatment of the child in the family will have a direct impact on the child's immediate social relationships and those in the wider world. Rather, the research is placed in a more appropriate, ecological perspective, that indicates that aspects of the child's life within the family will have connections with what happens outside the family, and what happens outside the family will have links with what happens within it. One study, for example, found that maltreated children differed from non-maltreated children in their conceptions of interpersonal relationships (Dean et al, 1986) and another, using a large sample of children aged 8–10, found that rejected children (in terms of peer nominations) were more likely to have a self-reported negative outcome than others (Kupersmidt and Patterson, 1991).

In a similar way to the research on the network characteristics and wider social relationships of parents, as this research has become more sophisticated more specific aspects of relationships have been examined. Howe and Parke (2001), for instance, looked at the difference between abused children's general popularity with classmates and their success in close friendships. They also examined what they refer to as the 'specific interactional' qualities of abused children's friendships and their links to loneliness. They found that, while abused children were not rated significantly lower sociometrically (eg, in terms of positive perspectives from peers) and that they did not differ significantly on measures of 'friendship quality' (eg, such as resolving conflicts and helping each other), they were perceived to be more negative, and less proactive, in their relations with peers.

The effects of residential mobility

Whilst there has been little research into the significance of residential mobility for children's social networks, it is likely that high rates of mobility will have a damaging impact. A child's sense of identity and security is likely to be affected by moving. Not only can local networks of friendship be broken up, but also the networks associated with schools may be disrupted. In addition, the familiarity and security of place may be lost.

Much, of course, will depend on the parents' ability to help the child cope with such moves, illustrating an important interaction between parenting capacity and structural factors.

The most extreme examples of this are likely to be experienced by refugee and asylum-seeking families and families that experience homelessness. As will be discussed in the chapter on *housing*, for example, becoming homeless will often involve a move from the current area of residence, with a consequent disruption to the social integration of the child.

The child or young person and deviant or delinquent peer groups

It is important to recognise that it is not only the positive aspects of support and acceptance that are important in looking at the child's and adolescent's involvement in social relationships outside the family.

There has long been a literature in the sociology of crime and delinquency, which focuses, in effect, on the child's and adolescent's social integration with anti-social peers (see, for instance, Gill, 1977 and Downes and Rock, 1998). This literature alerts us to the fact that delinquency, far from being an indication of a lack of social integration, may be evidence of a high level of integration – but crucially social integration into a deviant world.

In looking at this literature it is important to recognise that it focuses on an older age range than the majority of the studies referred to above, with delinquent behaviour apparently peaking in the mid-teenage years.

There are three key themes in this body of literature.

- Juvenile delinquency can be related to social disorganisation at a neighbourhood and community level – the neighbourhood or community does not have a clear set of normative controls against deviant or delinquent activity.

- Subcultures, particularly those of adolescent males, develop which incorporate a deviant set of norms. Delinquent activity is condoned or positively regarded within these subcultures.

- The degree of 'social integration' of the child or adolescent into these subcultures will strongly influence the extent of deviant or delinquent activity.

For assessment purposes, this perspective requires that the potentially negative and damaging aspects of social integration are fully explored, alongside the positive aspects that have been discussed above.

Again, it is necessary to explore the relationship between the two worlds of the child or adolescent. How, for instance, do the values of the family relate to and impact on the values of the outside social world? There is significant evidence, for example, of the way in which the family and the outside world can interact to protect the child from the influences of a delinquent subculture. In the mid-1970s Wilson and Herbert (1978) in the UK showed that, even in 'delinquent areas', particular styles of parenting could protect children from involvement in delinquency. More recently, in the US, Furstenberg (1999) has looked at family influences on adolescent lives and explored how and why some young people are able to overcome social adversity. Both of these studies go to the heart of the ecological perspective because they show how family, child and environmental factors interact and influence each other.

Issues for assessment

This necessarily limited review has aimed to highlight the main areas of research, which point to questions to guide the assessment of families and children in relation to social integration. Overall, the picture that emerges is of the significance of relationships outside the immediate family as the child grows and develops. These relationships will be important from the early pre-school days in terms of the level of contact and the diversity of experiences involved. Also, from an early stage, the child's own contacts in nursery and pre-school groups will be of significance. As the child grows, school and neighbourhood peer groups will become more important. Their nature and degree of supportiveness will play a role in the child's developing sense of self. Rejection by other children can lead to either internalised difficulties, such as depression, or externalised difficulties, such as behaviour problems. The complex connections between the family and the external social world will also be significant. If, for instance, there is mistreatment within the family, this is likely to have implications for the child's sense of confidence outside the family.

Social integration is a central concept for workers undertaking the assessment of children in need from an ecological perspective. An analysis of the social integration of the child into the immediate and wider family, neighbourhood and formal institutions, such as the school, will highlight and identify many of the strengths and pressures which the child is experiencing.

These again should not be considered in isolation. As with all the other assessment categories within the framework, it is crucial to see the links and interconnections between the categories. To fail to do this undermines the ecological approach to assessment.

The family's social integration will, for instance, in part be influenced by local community resources. Children and parents who are living in neighbourhoods with few community resources will be denied opportunities for making contact with others.

Equally, the family's social integration will be influenced by *housing* availability and allocation policies. For instance if a family is offered accommodation only in areas where they have few contacts and networks this will very significantly affect their level of social integration. In this there may be particular issues for black and mixed-race families. If the only available accommodation is on mainly white estates, black and dual-heritage children may be particularly disadvantaged in terms of social integration. In the chapter on housing we will also examine the very extreme impact on children's social integration that homelessness can have.

Income and family finances will also be important in determining the levels and characteristics of social integration. Those families with few financial resources are likely to have fewer opportunities for developing contact. Practitioners will come across many situations in which the family's lack of money precludes trips, parties, and holidays, for example, which other children take for granted.

And of course there are links between employment and levels of social integration. Not only will networks be central in obtaining employment but also those in employment are likely to have more extended networks.

There will also be connections to wider family members. The child and parent living in a setting of strong contact with wider family members are also likely to have their more general links into the community enhanced.

It is important to recognise that effective assessments of social integration can only be achieved if the worker has an understanding of the community and neighbourhood of which the child is a part, and of the cultural norms surrounding children within those communities and neighbourhoods.

References

Baldwin, N and Carruthers, L (1998) *Developing Neighbourhood Support and Child Protection Strategies*. Aldershot: Ashgate Publishing

Belle D (1982) Social ties and social support. In D Belle (ed) *Lives in Stress*, pp133–44. Beverly Hills, CA: Sage

Bulkley, J (2000) *Culture's Influence on Parents and Children. The Role of Ethnicity and Parenting and Child Competence in African American and European American Families*. Unpublished dissertation, University of Oregon, quoted in Deater-Deckard (2001) as below

Buysse, W (1997) Behaviour problems and relationships with family and peers during adolescence. *Journal of Adolescence*, **20**, 645–59

Cochran, M and Riley, D (1990) The social networks of six-year-olds: context, content and consequence. In Cochran *et al* (1990) *Extending Families: The Social Networks of Parents and their Children*, Cambridge: Cambridge University Press

Coleman, JS (1988) Social capital in the creation of human capital. *American Journal of Sociology*, **94 (suppl)**, 595–620

Coohey, C (1996) Child mistreatment; testing the social isolation hypothesis. *Child Abuse and Neglect*, **20**(3), 241–54

Cotterill, AM (1988) Geographic distribution of child abuse in an inner-city borough. *Child Abuse and Neglect*, **12**, 461–7

Crittenden PM (1985) Social networks, quality of child rearing and child development. *Child Development*, **56**, 1299–313

Crnic, KA, Greenberg, MT, Robinson, NM, Ragozin, AS (1984) Maternal stress and social support. Effects on the mother-infant relationship from birth to eighteen months. *American Journal of Orthopsychiatry*, **54**, 224–35

Dean, A, Malik, M, Richards, W, Stringer, S (1986) Effects of parental maltreatment on children's conceptions of interpersonal relationships. *Developmental Psychology*, **24**, 776–81, quoted in Cochran and Riley (1990), as above

Deater-Deckard, K (2001) Annotation: recent research examining the role of peer relationships in the development of psychopathology. *Journal of Child Psychology and Psychiatry*, **42**(5), 565–79

Department of Health (2000) *Framework for the Assessment of Children in Need and their Families*. London: The Stationery Office

Downes, D and Rock, P (1998) *Understanding Deviance*. Oxford: Oxford University Press

Dunn, J (1993) *Young Children's Close Relationships*. Newbury Park, CA: Sage

Dunn, J and Mcguire, S (1992) Sibling and peer relationships in childhood. *Journal of Child Psychology and Psychiatry*, **33**(1), 67–105

Fiering, C and Lewis, M (1981) The social networks of three year old children. Paper presented at the biennial meeting of the Society for Research in Child Development, Boston, quoted in Cochran and Riley (1990), as above

Fischer, C (1982) *To Dwell Among Friends: Personal Networks in Town and City*. Chicago: Chicago University Press

Furstenberg, F (1999) *Managing to Make It: Urban families and adolescent success*. Chicago: University of Chicago Press

Garbarino, J and Crouter, A (1978) Defining the community context of parent-child relations: the correlates of child mistreatment. *Child Development*, **49**, 604–16

Garbarino, J and Sherman, D (1980) High-risk neighbourhoods and high-risk families: the human ecology of child mistreatment. *Child Development*, **51**, 188–98

Gardner, R (1992) *Supporting Families: Preventive social work in practice*. London: National Children's Bureau

Gibbons, J (1990) *Family Support and Prevention: Studies in local areas*. London: HMSO

Gill, O (1977) *Luke Street, housing policy, conflict and the creation of the delinquent area*. Basingstoke: Macmillan

Gill, O, Tanner, C, Bland, L (2000) *Family Support: Strengths and pressures in a 'high risk' neighbourhood*. Barkingside: Barnardo's

Gilroy, P (1987) *There Ain't No Black in the Union Jack*. London: Hutchinson

Hartup, WW (1996) The company they keep: friendships and their developmental significance. *Child Development*, **67**, 1–13

Howe, TR and Parke, RD (2001) Friendship quality and sociometric status: between group differences and links to loneliness in severely abused and non-abused children. *Child Abuse and Neglect*, **25**, 585–606

Howes, C (1988) *Peer Interactions of Young Children*, Monographs of the Society for Research in Child Development, 53 (1, Serial No. 217) quoted in MC Smith, (1995), A preliminary description of Non-school-based friendship in young high-risk children. *Child Abuse and Neglect*, **19**(12), 1497–511

Jack, G (2000) Ecological Influences on parenting and child development. *British Journal of Social Work*, **30**, 703–20

Kupersmidt, J and Patterson, C (1991) Childhood peer rejection, aggression, withdrawal and perceived competence as predictors of self-reported behaviour problems in pre-adolescence. *Journal of Abnormal Child Psychology*, **19**, 427–49

Maluccio, AN (1989) Research perspectives on social support systems for families and children. *Journal of Applied Social Sciences*, **13**(2) (Spring/Summer)

Moncher, F (1995) Social isolation and child abuse risk. *The Journal of Contemporary Human Services*, September

Packman, J with Randall, J and Jacques, N (1986), *Who Needs Care? Social work decisions about children*. Oxford: Blackwell

Pavis, S, Platt, S, Hubbard, G (2000) *Young People in Rural Scotland: Pathways to social inclusion and exclusion.* York: York Publishing Services (for Joseph Rowntree Foundation)

Polansky, N, Gaudin, J, Ammons, P, David, K (1985) The psychological ecology of the neglectful mother, *Journal of Child Abuse and Neglect*, **9**, 265–75

Puttnam, RD (1993) *Making Democracy Work: Civic traditions in modern Italy.* Princeton, NJ: Princeton University Press

Reid, M et al (1989) 'My family and friends': 6–12-year-old children's perceptions of social support. *Child Development*, **60**, 896–910

Ridge, T (2002) *Childhood Poverty and Social Exclusion.* Bristol: The Policy Press

Ridge, T and Davis, J (1997) *Same Scenery, Different Lifestyle. Rural children on a low income.* London: The Children's Society

Sampson, R, Morenoff, JD, Earls, F (1999) Beyond social capital: spatial dynamics of collective efficacy for children. *American Sociological Review*, **64**, 633–60

Simcha-Fagan, O and Schwartz, J (1986) Neighbourhood and delinquency: an assessment of contextual effects. *Criminology*, **24**(4), 667–703

Starr, RH (1982) A research based approach to the prediction of child abuse. In RH Starr (ed) *Child Abuse Prediction*, pp105–34. Cambridge, MA: Ballinger

Stocker, C (1994) Children's perceptions of relationships with siblings, friends and mothers: compensatory processes and links with adjustment. *Journal of Child Psychology and Psychiatry*, **35**(8) 1447–59

Thompson, R (1995) *Preventing Child Mistreatment through Social Support.: A critical analysis.* California: Sage

Tracey, E and Whittaker, JK (1987) The evidence base for social support interventions in child and family practice: emerging issues for research and practice. *Children and Youth Services Review*, **9**, 249–70 quoted in Maluccio AN (1989), as above

Vinson, T, Baldry, E, Hargreaves, J (1996). Neighbourhoods, networks and child abuse. *British Journal of Social Work*, **26**, 243–53

Werner, E (1995) Resilience in development. *Current Directions in Psychological Science*, American Psychological Society, **4**(5), 81–5

Williams, F (1993) Women and community. In J Bornat, C Pereira, D Pilgrim and F Williams (eds) *Community Care – A reader*, pp33–42. Basingstoke: Macmillan

Wilson, H and Herbert, G (1978) *Parents and Children in the Inner City.* London: Routledge

Income 4

This chapter draws on a strong UK research base, as well as considerable practice experience, to identify the issues that are most important to understand in assessing a family's income. It begins by considering the different ways that family income and levels of poverty are measured and experienced by different family members, including the different access that men, women, and children have to family income. It then goes on to highlight the rising levels of poverty and inequality evident in the UK over the past 25 years, and the way that family income can vary in relation to such factors as geographical location, ethnic background, disability (of parents and children), and family structure. This is followed by a detailed examination of the wide range of ways that lack of sufficient income can affect parenting capacity and children's development, emphasising the interactions between income and other dimensions within the assessment triangle. The chapter concludes with a consideration of what has been termed 'poverty blindness' amongst child welfare workers and organisations, and a summary of the main issues for assessment in relation to income.

Measurement of sufficiency to meet needs

The degree to which a family's level of income is sufficient to meet their needs depends on a wide range of factors, including: their housing costs; levels of debt; family composition; the health, disability, age and gender of individual members; and their geographical location. Those assessing these matters also need to be aware of how financial resources are distributed within households, and the levels of support available from wider family members, friends and neighbours. Furthermore, the pattern of income, over time, will need to be considered. For example, whilst a new job may currently be providing sufficient income to meet the family's immediate needs, sustained or repeated periods of poverty in the past may have seriously depleted household resources or raised the levels of debt.

In order to quantify overall levels of income for different groups, within a given population, researchers and governments have developed a number of different measures. The most commonly used measures involve the use of a poverty threshold, either below 50 per cent of the mean income of the country (normally used within the EU) or 60 per cent of the median income (now used by the UK government). These calculations can be presented either before or after housing costs have been taken into account. Another well-established approach uses population surveys to estimate the costs of providing what are generally considered to be the necessities of family life, such as the 'Breadline Index' (Mack and Lansley, 1985; Gordon and Pantazis, 1997).

Rising poverty and inequality in the UK

Whatever measure of income is used, it is well known that the proportion of the UK population living in poor households has risen significantly in recent times. The number of people living in households with less than half the average income, after housing costs, was more than 14 million in 1998/99, more than double the figure in the early 1980s (Rahman *et al*, 2000). Families with children (especially lone-parent families) have been particularly affected by this growing impoverishment, with approximately one third of all children in the UK living in poor households at the start of the twenty-first century, a higher proportion than in any other EU country (Eurostat, 2000). These rises in poverty reflect an increasingly unequal society in which the richest 20 per cent of the population received 45 per cent of national income (after tax) in 1999/2000. This compares to only 6 per cent of national income received by the poorest fifth of the population (Office for National Statistics, 2001). The same source reveals that the most widely used index of income inequality, known as the Gini Coefficient (where 0 per cent represents complete equality of income), has reached an all-time high in the UK, standing at 40 per cent in 1999/2000, having risen from 27 per cent in 1975.

Income support levels represent the basic safety net under which families should not fall. However, there is now substantial evidence that a large number of families are surviving on incomes below these levels, primarily because of loans from the Social Fund and the repayment of other debts. For assessment purposes, it is essential to understand the characteristics of routine debts and the way in which these impact on families. The sorts of debts incurred by people on benefits include repayments to catalogue companies, loan sharks, finance companies, and members of their wider families. One important aspect of this is that poor people often pay very high rates of interest on their loans. The majority of European countries have a ceiling on the interest that can be charged on credit. However, this is not the case in the UK, leading to a situation in which those least able to afford a loan will often pay the most for it. The scale of the commercial debt problem for poor families is indicated by the fact that Provident Financial, which specialises in providing credit for otherwise financially excluded people, has a UK client base of some 1.6 million people (*Guardian*, 2002).

All of these sources of debt are important and need to be taken into account in assessing the financial stresses that the family is experiencing. However, for many families, the most significant routine debt is likely to be repayments to the Social Fund. The majority of payments from the Social Fund are made as loans, with a weekly amount deducted from claimants' benefit. Research and practice experience both indicate that many families, particularly the most hard-pressed, are living below income support levels. The following, for instance, is a routine case (2001–2002 rates) described in Gill (2001).

> Becky Knight lives on a large peripheral city estate. She is a lone parent with one child aged 4 years. Her Income Support entitlement is £100.40 per week, including her Child Benefit. However, just before her child was born Becky was given temporary accommodation in a housing association flat. She received a £400 crisis loan to help her to set up home in the flat. She started paying back the loan at £11 a week – an amount she has continued to pay throughout the subsequent four years because she has taken out further loans to pay for essential items. Her weekly income is therefore significantly below the Income Support level.

Concern about the Social Fund is widespread, with the Select Committee on Social Security (2001) concluding, 'the present Social Fund system is working against the Government's key aim of reducing child poverty. Our inquiry has shown that in its present form the discretionary Social Fund is adding to the poverty and social exclusion of families with children by, in many cases, denying them access to basic necessities and increasing their indebtedness.' Because of the Social Fund, then, families routinely have to live below the poverty line. This point is powerfully made by Craig (2001), who argues that 'the fund officially sanctions the breaking of the Beveridge safety net. Social Fund loans take claimants' income 15 per cent (and sometimes more) below the official poverty line.'

The Labour government elected in 1997 stated that it wished to eliminate child poverty within 20 years. The initiatives that have been introduced since then, including the Working Families Tax Credit, increases to benefit levels, and the minimum wage legislation, have so far lifted only about 500,000 children out of poverty (between 1996/97 and 2000/01). This is a fall from 4.4 million to 3.9 million children (Department for Work and Pensions, 2002). Furthermore, the majority of the children lifted out of poverty by these measures are likely to have been living in households with incomes closest to the poverty threshold, most of whom may only have been moved just above the threshold by the measures taken so far (Piachaud and Sutherland, 2000). Success in maintaining these households above the poverty line, and in reaching other families living in deeper poverty, will require continued national economic growth, further social policy initiatives, and redistributive tax and benefit changes for many years to come.

Variations in poverty and income

As already mentioned, an important aspect of the assessment of family incomes is the pattern of income over time. At one extreme, experiences of poverty can be transient, which is not likely to have long-term effects, through recurrent and persistent poverty, to permanent poverty, at the other extreme, which will almost certainly have adverse long-term effects on both adults and children (Goodman, Johnson and Webb, 1997). A recent Treasury report estimated that as many as a quarter of the children now being born into poor households are likely to experience permanent poverty, without further social and economic reform (HM Treasury, 1999).

Length of time on benefit may also play an important role in shaping the family's current financial position and the resources it has for children. It is likely that the cumulative effects of income deprivation will create increasing problems for families. One of the most important reasons for this is that the family is likely to accumulate larger debts the longer it has been dependent on benefits. Also, length of time on benefit is likely to impact on the quality of the home environment, in terms of such things as the state of repair of furnishings and equipment, and the purchase of clothing and age-appropriate toys for children.

Other significant factors include geographical location, ethnic background and disability. Using the Breadline Index, the most impoverished regions of the UK are found in Inner London, Strathclyde, Tyne and Wear, and North West England. For example, 43 per cent of Inner London's 1.5 million children were living in poor households in 1999/2000, compared to the national average of 32 per cent (Department for Work and Pensions, 2001). However, national data of this kind tend to mask income inequalities, both between different areas in the same region, and between different groups, such as families with young children, lone parents, minority ethnic communities, childless couples, and older people, in the same areas (Lee and Murie, 1997). Some families will live in areas where *community resources* are extensive. In these areas there may, for instance, be sources of cheap, good quality food, credit unions and welfare rights advice agencies. Families living in other areas may, however, be dependent on more expensive corner-shop provision, without sources of financial advice and support. It is also important not to focus attention exclusively on urban areas, simply because of their higher density of population. There is growing awareness and concern about the particular problems faced by those living in rural poverty, including limited opportunities to access well-paid employment, combined with high transport costs and isolation from mainstream services (Pavis, Platt and Hubbard, 2000; Craig and Manthorpe, 2000). In a rural setting, families may have to make long journeys to buy food, so incurring additional costs, for often expensive public transport, on top of the cost of the food itself.

Insufficient income to meet family needs is also a particular problem for households that include a child with a disability or chronic illness. It has been estimated, for example, that the costs involved in caring for a severely disabled child are three times greater than those for a non-disabled child. However, benefit levels fall up to 50 per cent short of meeting the additional costs involved, and opportunities for increasing income through paid *employment* are more restricted for families with disabled children (Dobson and Middleton, 1998). These problems are particularly acute for minority ethnic families, whose take-up of benefits is lower than other families', and for whom rates of unemployment and other indices of deprivation are generally much higher than the rest of the population. Families of Pakistani and Bangladeshi origin are particularly disadvantaged, consistently being found to be among the poorest people living in the UK (Berthoud, 1998; Smaje, 1995; Platt and Noble, 1999).

Finally, family composition also plays an important role in determining whether household income is sufficient to meet family needs. Family size obviously plays a part here, and lone parents (who are overwhelmingly women) are particularly vulnerable to poverty. In the UK, two-thirds of children in lone-parent households are poor, compared to only a quarter of children in two-parent households (Gregg, Harkness and Machin, 1999). Although recent government initiatives have attempted to improve the income of lone parents, limited access to affordable childcare is still a major impediment for many such families. Despite the introduction of childcare tax credits, it was estimated that only 13 per cent of all parents with dependent children could afford to use full-time childcare provision in 2001 (Daycare Trust, 2001).

Effects of poverty on children and families

Using relative measures of poverty, at a time when earnings are rising, it can be argued that even families on less than half the average income should be able to manage adequately. This is where theories about a 'culture of poverty' and an 'underclass' (Murray, 1990) originate, suggesting that it is the attitudes, behaviour, aspirations, and values of poor people that are at the root of their problems, rather than access to financial resources *per se*. Whilst there is evidence of some effect of growing up in poverty on children's beliefs, attitudes and behaviour (eg Shropshire and Middleton, 1999), nevertheless most people living in impoverished circumstances share similar aspirations to the rest of society. These include the desire for a job, a decent home, and sufficient income to cover their bills, with a little money spare for extras or savings (Kempson, 1996). Similar findings emerged from an in-depth study of young people in a disadvantaged neighbourhood in north-east England. Few wanted to live on benefits, and most aspired to get a 'proper job' that was stable and rewarding (Johnston et al, 2000). In general, the preferred 'solution' for most adults living in poverty is well-paid and secure employment (Kempson, Bryson and Rowlingson, 1994; Middleton, Ashworth and Braithwaite, 1997).

A great deal of everyday practice experience testifies to the fact that the physical home environment of families on benefit may be inadequate, in many respects, for the appropriate care of children. This may take such forms as a lack of carpeting, kitchen appliances that are faulty, badly worn furniture, and a lack of books and toys. In the most extreme situations, families may even be disconnected from essential services. There is also considerable research and practice experience which shows that children and adults in income-deprived families are likely to experience inferior diets. This may take the form of not having three decent meals a day or it may mean having too much fat and sugar, or inadequate amounts of fresh fruit and vegetables in the diet.

An in-depth study of 74 low-income families living on benefits found that financial worries were a constant preoccupation, with spending on food, rent and fuel prioritised over clothes, shoes, and any personal needs. The only area of flexibility in household budgets tended to be spending on food, with parents invariably putting their children's needs first and shopping around for the cheapest food. Social activities, holidays, and home maintenance were all curtailed, and family members were forced to spend a lot of their time together, placing a strain on relationships in the context of limited resources. Women carried a heavy burden for managing scarce resources, and evidence of irresponsible spending was rare. Informal help, in cash and in kind, was common amongst relatives and friends, with an element of reciprocity being an important underpinning principle in many exchanges. The most common source and direction of help was from mothers to their adult children (Kempson, Bryson and Rowlingson, 1994; Kempson, 1996).

In fact, as we suggested in the opening to this chapter, support from *wider family* networks can make a very significant difference to the financial position of income-deprived families. Grandparents may, for instance, help parents out by lending money or helping with transport. Equally importantly, they may be a source of treats and activities for children. These sorts of assistance are common, even if the parents have separated. Research among parents in Bristol revealed that some paternal grandparents remained very significantly supportive of their grandchildren, even after their own son had left the family home (Gill *et al*, 2000). Practice experience, demonstrates the way that supportive *wider family* networks can significantly ameliorate the financial stresses on families. Those parents with few supports may be operating in significantly more stressful financial circumstances.

As indicated above, children and parents living in income-deprived families do not usually have the money for treats and special family events. They lack the financial resources to 'do nice things together', in a way that more advantaged families take for granted. The most obvious example of this is that, without the help of wider networks, families in income-deprived households are unlikely to be able to go on holiday together. This means that children in poor families do not have as wide an experience of different environments and activities as do their peers in more favoured families. There are many practice examples that illustrate this. For instance, a Barnardo's worker recently arranged a trip to a local theatre to see a children's show. Afterwards a lone parent with four children said it was the first time that she had ever been able to do something nice with all of her children together. Without events and activities to look forward to, the stresses of family life are increased and family relationships are undermined.

Living in an income-deprived family also has implications for children's *social integration*, the richness of their social world, and their self-esteem. These sorts of effects are evident in the following quote, from a 13-year-old girl living on a housing estate in an inner-city area of Bristol, one of a group of 40 children interviewed as part of a study of childhood poverty:

'You can't do as much, and I don't like my clothes and that, so I don't really get to do much or do stuff like my friends are doing ... I am worried about what people think of me, like they think I am sad or something.' (Ridge, 2002)

Children living in impoverished households are also less likely to have other children to come to visit and play at home, or to have birthday parties. Poverty also impacts on the family's ability to share in childcare arrangements, which may further restrict the child's social world. For example, particularly in rural settings, parents will often develop reciprocal transport arrangements to facilitate trips to activities, such as Brownies and swimming. If parents do not have their own means of transport, involvement in the social relationships that evolve from these arrangements will be minimised. It is also more difficult for children in income-deprived families to attend youth and other leisure clubs on a regular basis, because of the costs involved. For instance, in a market town, where Barnardo's is engaged in anti-poverty work, such children can rarely afford to go to the expensive, local swimming pool. Practice experience also suggests that children from income-deprived families often do not have the up-to-date, stylish goods by which children tend to judge one another and, to an extent, that they also use to judge themselves. This is illustrated by a mother talking about her daughter having to have a second-hand bike:

'She is the only one who hasn't got a scooter around here. She's got a bike which was her sister's. It's old-fashioned. All of her friends have got these suspension ones or whatever.' (Gill, 2001)

Being dependent on income support may also make it problematic for children to participate fully and equally in school activities. This can happen at a number of levels. First of all, parents may find the purchase of school uniform a major drain on their financial resources. Research has shown the inadequacy of school uniform grants and the very uneven availability of these grants (NACAB, 2001) Nearly a third of local education authorities provided no assistance at all with school uniform costs for families on low incomes and, in real terms, the level of financial assistance declined between 1990 and 2000. In Bristol, for instance, the maximum school uniform grant awarded is £30 per child (2001) and this is discretionary, depending on the particular circumstances of the family. The NACAB research found that the minimum cost of school uniform for a child moving onto secondary school was £105. Secondly, although parents on income support may be entitled to free school meals, there is evidence that, because of the stigma involved, some children do not receive them (CPAG, 2000). This will obviously have implications for the child's diet, which, in turn, may have an impact on their educational attainment. It is also important to recognise that entitlement to free school meals is restricted to children whose families are dependent on income support. The children of working parents who are on low wages do not receive free school meals. Thirdly, there is considerable practice experience that many children whose families are dependent on benefits are not able to go on school trips and holidays and are therefore not able to participate fully in the opportunities of their schooling.

The clearest research evidence of the long-term effects of living without sufficient income on individual development and well-being is provided by the extensive research literature examining health inequalities (Wilkinson, 1996; Nazroo, 1997). It is a sad fact that, in the UK, 'The health of people in the more affluent areas of the country is among the best in the developed world, but the health of the most disadvantaged rivals the worst.' (CPAG, 2000–2002). One of the most recent reviews of the evidence on health inequalities in the UK is provided by the government-commissioned report by Sir Donald Acheson, published in 1998. This confirmed the clear health gradients, from rich to poor, that exist in the UK for virtually all diseases and causes of death. For example, the likelihood of men aged 45 to 64 years having a life-limiting chronic illness rises from 17 per cent for those in the professional classes, to 48 per cent for those in the unskilled classes. Furthermore, the intergenerational effects of poverty are revealed by the way in which pregnant women in disadvantaged groups are more likely to be undernourished, and more likely to go on to have low-birthweight babies who, in turn, are at increased risk of developing heart disease in later life (*Guardian*, 1998). Family poverty, experienced early in life, also has a profound effect on children's development. A recent Treasury report found that, as early as 22 months of age, children from the poorest families are already 14 per cent lower on an educational development scale than those from the richest families (HM Treasury, 1999). To make matters worse, work at Essex University has revealed that pre-school children have a disproportionately high risk of experiencing repeated periods of poverty – twice that of the population as a whole (*Guardian*, 2000).

Social work's attitudes and responses

If poverty is such an important factor in family functioning and children's development, it would be reasonable to assume that it would be high on the agenda of all social work agencies. As many as nine out of ten users of social work services are benefit claimants, and numerous studies and child-abuse inquiries have demonstrated the strong associations between family poverty and the numbers of both children looked after by local authorities and cases of reported child abuse (Becker, 1997).

Unfortunately, several studies of local authority social workers' attitudes towards poverty and poor people have revealed ambivalence, confusion, lack of awareness ('poverty blindness') and reluctance to get involved (Clark and Davis, 1997; Becker, 1997; Dowling, 1999). For example, in a survey of social workers in four local authorities, asked to identify the causes of the needs of 40 children for whom they were responsible, family poverty was not identified as the main cause of need for any of them. Poverty was only mentioned at all, as a contributory cause of need, in under 30 per cent of cases (Lister, 2001). Too often, studies of local-authority social workers reveal a limited awareness of poverty as a social and structural, rather than a personal and individual, problem, reflecting wider societal and historical attitudes towards poverty in the UK (Jones and Novak, 1999; Becker, 1997). Organisational and individual commitment to actively engage in anti-poverty work are often absent, and attempts to maximise the income of poor households are far from routine. It has largely been left to other local authority staff and voluntary social work agencies, such as Barnardo's, to develop more active strategies for combating family poverty. These include support for anti-poverty campaigning, the development of credit unions and food co-operatives, the provision of affordable childcare, and the social and economic regeneration of local neighbourhoods (McLeod and Bywaters, 2000).

Issues for assessment

Most assessments of family finances, relating to children in need, confine themselves primarily to *quantitative* issues, such as the level of income coming in to a household, and the level of outgoings, including debts. For example, the Department of Health's Core Assessment forms ask simple 'yes/no' questions about whether the family are: receiving all the benefits to which they are entitled; paying their household bills regularly; managing on their income; worried about their future financial commitments, including debt repayments. Whilst this sort of information provides an adequate starting point, it does not go anything like far enough in ensuring an accurate picture of the impact of income insufficiency on the family's functioning, and on the individual children's development. First of all, there may be a need to gather much more detailed information about a family's financial circumstances. For example, for families in serious financial trouble, workers might need to understand the full extent of the family's debts, including the total weekly payments that they are required to make, over what time span, and incurring what penalties for non- or late payment. If the debts include repayments to the Social Fund, have the weekly instalments been negotiated to be as low as possible? Potential sources of income also need to be maximised, ensuring not only that benefit entitlement is being received, but also helping the family to explore other sources of financial support that might be available to them, such as credit union loans or charitable grants, if these are acceptable to the family.

However, evidence reviewed here has also pointed to a wide range of other implications of income insufficiency that may need to be taken into account in assessments. The starting point would have to be the worker's and the agency's attitudes and policies in relation to issues of poverty. Workers need to consider whether the people they are in contact with who are living in poor households are viewed as active partners in identifying and finding solutions to their difficulties, or if they are treated more as passive objects of the possible largesse of welfare agencies. Does their agency have clear anti-poverty strategies and, if so, how effectively are they monitored and communicated to its employees and service users? Are staff required to undergo poverty awareness training and are attitudes and practices monitored within supervision and staff development processes? Do front-line staff and their managers consider direct involvement in anti-poverty work to be a part of their everyday duties and responsibilities, or something that 'other people' do? Within an overall awareness of the social and structural causes of poverty, workers and agencies also need to develop strategies to focus their attentions on identifying and supporting particularly vulnerable groups. Research evidence consistently shows that families with children, especially large families, lone-parent families, and households with young children, or of minority ethnic (especially Pakistani and Bangladeshi) origin, or where children or adults have disabilities, are all particularly vulnerable to experiencing serious shortfalls in income sufficient to meet their needs. Reconstituted families may also be particularly vulnerable if adult members are financially responsible for more than one household of dependent children.

Assessments of financial circumstances also need to incorporate a temporal dimension. We have seen that poverty can occur on a spectrum from a short-lived, transient experience or something that recurs frequently, through to the point where it can be termed persistent or even permanent. The research evidence supports the commonsense assumption that the damaging effects of poverty on families are greater, the deeper the poverty, and the longer it lasts. It also appears that young children, in their pre-school years, are particularly vulnerable to the effects of poverty on their development, whilst at the same time living in households that are more likely to experience poverty than the general population. Workers therefore need to know how long a family has been living on benefits or a very low income. If the family has experienced persistent or permanent poverty, over a significant period of time, this is likely to have had a damaging impact on the physical quality of the home environment, the indebtedness of the family, and the children's full participation or attainment at school, their networks of social relationships, and their diet. The worker undertaking the assessment may also want to know if children are able to participate in activities outside the household and to go on trips to the cinema, bowling alley, shops and swimming baths, either with friends or with other members of the family. Has the family ever had a holiday together and can they rely on their *wider family* to help them provide occasional treats? Does the child have friends back to the house to play, for a meal, or to sleep over? Can the parents participate in reciprocal childcare arrangements and provide the toys or style goods that other children of the same age might possess?

Attention has also been drawn to the experience of poverty within particular households. A focus on the qualitative aspects of poverty is called for here, recognising that each person is a unique individual, with their own characteristics, *family history* and experiences, beliefs, skills and coping mechanisms. Workers may need to understand how each member of a particular family reacts to the pressures of life on a low income and the effects that their situation is having on their self-esteem, health, and thinking. People need the opportunity to express their own feelings and to construct their own understanding of their lives, in ways that are meaningful to themselves. Factors such as age, gender, and culture are all likely to be significant in determining how household resources are distributed and in creating unique perspectives for individual members of households experiencing poverty. Whilst one member of a household might have been relatively protected from some of the most harmful effects of poverty and be optimistic about their own prospects for the future, another member of the same household might be feeling very depressed and trapped within an apparently never-ending downward spiral. This means listening to children, as well as adults, giving them an opportunity to say what it is like to be poor, from their own perspective. Workers may also need to explore the extent to which *wider family* members help out financially and the form that any help takes (eg loans, transport costs, gifts, help in kind, and direct support of grandchildren including presents, treats and holidays).

Finally, the research evidence points to the importance of viewing family poverty in its wider social and environmental context. Geographical location can be an important factor, both in the distribution of overall levels of poverty and in the particular challenges faced by individual households. How supportive and accessible are parents and wider family members, as well as close friends and other social network members? What is the quality and accessibility of mainstream resources, such as childcare, schools, after-school resources, shops, family centres, youth clubs, adult education classes and leisure facilities? If rurality is an issue, what are the transport services like and how affordable are they for people living on low incomes? Is a lack of *social integration* reinforcing the effects of poverty, and combining to undermine parenting capacity and child development? Do *community resources*, such as mutual-interest and self-help groups and organisations, exist within the locality that might be supportive of families with children? Is the local area a safe place for children to play and form friendships, or are crime, anti-social behaviour and drug-use at high levels, requiring more intense parental supervision, and restrictions on children's freedom? Whilst many of these wider social and environmental issues are not *directly* related to income, per se, it is the way that they interact with households living in poverty that is the essence of the ecological model and that needs to be taken into account when assessing income. Families living in poverty are far more likely to be exposed to higher levels of environmental risk with fewer supportive resources to call upon.

References

Becker, S (1997) *Responding to Poverty: The politics of cash and care*. Harlow: Longman

Berthoud, R (1998) *The Incomes of Ethnic Minorities* (98-1). University of Essex: Institute for Social and Economic Research

Clark, B and Davis, A (1997) When money's too tight to mention. *Professional Social Work*, March, 12–13

Craig, G and Manthorpe, J (2000) *Fresh Fields: Rural social care – research, policy, and practice agendas*. York: Joseph Rowntree Foundation

Child Poverty Action Group (CPAG) (2000–2002) *Tackling Inequalities in Health*. http://www.cpag.org.uk/info/Poverty articles/Poverty110/health.htm

Craig, G (2001) Submission to the Select Committee on Social Security. Reported in: Select Committee on Social Security. *The Social Fund: Third Report of the Select Committee on Social Security*. London: The Stationery Office

Daycare Trust (2001) *The Price Parents Pay*. London: The Daycare Trust

Department for Work and Pensions (2001) *Survey of Households with Below Average Income in 1999–2000*. London: The Stationery Office

Department for Work and Pensions (2002) *Households Below Average Income 1994/5 – 2001*, http://www.dwp.gov.uk

Dobson, B and Middleton, S (1998) *Paying to Care: The cost of childhood disability*. York: York Publishing Services (for JRF)

Dowling, M (1999) *Social Work and Poverty: Attitudes and actions*. Aldershot: Ashgate

Gill, O (2001) *Invisible Children: Child and family poverty in Bristol, Bath, Gloucestershire, Somerset and Wiltshire*. Barkingside: Barnardo's

Gill, O, Tanner, C, Bland, L (2000) *Family Support: Strengths and pressures in a 'high risk' neighbourhood*. Barkingside: Barnardo's

Goodman, A, Johnson, P, Webb, S (1997) *Inequality in the UK*. Oxford: Oxford University Press

Gordon, D and Pantazis, C (eds) (1997) *Breadline Britain in the 1990s*. Aldershot: Ashgate

Gregg, P, Harkness, S, Machin, S (1999) *Child Development and Family Income*. York: Joseph Rowntree Foundation

Guardian (1998) Radical Reform Urge on Killer Poverty (The Acheson Report), 27 November, p3

Guardian (2000) Persistent Pest, 2 March, G2, p7

HM Treasury (1999) *Tackling Poverty and Extending Opportunity*. London: The Stationery Office

Johnston, L, Macdonald, R, Mason, P, Ridley, L, Webster, C (2000) *Snakes and Ladders: Young people, transitions and social exclusion*. Abingdon: The Policy Press (for JRF)

Jones, C and Novak, T (1999) *Poverty, Welfare and the Disciplinary State*. London: Routledge

Kempson, E (1996) *Life on a Low Income*. York: York Publishing Services (for JRF)

Kempson, E, Bryson, A, Rowlingson, K (1994) *Hard Times? How poor families make ends meet*. London, Policy Studies Institute

Lee, P and Murie, A (1997) *Poverty, Housing Tenure and Social Exclusion*. Bristol: The Policy Press

Lister, R (2001) The language of need: social workers describing the needs of children. In Department of Health, *Studies Informing the Framework for the Assessment of Children in Need and their Families*. London: The Stationery Office

Mack, J and Lansley, S (1985) *Poor Britain*. London: Allen and Unwin

McLeod, E and Bywaters, P (2000) *Social Work, Health and Equality*. London: Routledge

Middleton, S, Ashworth, K, Braithwaite, I (1997) *Small Fortunes: Spending on children, childhood poverty and parental sacrifice*. York: York Publishing Services (for JRF)

Murray, C (1990) *The Emerging British Underclass*. London: Institute of Economic Affairs

National Association of Citizens Advice Bureaux (2001) *Uniform Failure*. London: NACAB

Pavis, S, Platt, S, Hubbard, G (2000) *Young People in Rural Scotland: Pathways to Social Inclusion and Exclusion*. York: York Publishing Services (for JRF)

Piachaud, D and Sutherland, H (2000) *How Effective is the British Government's Attempt to Reduce Child Poverty?* CASE Paper 38 LSE/STICERD

Platt, L and Noble, M (1999) *Race, Place and Poverty: Ethnic groups and low income distribution*. York: York Publishing Services (for JRF)

Rahman, M, Palmer, G, Kenway, P, Howarth, C (2000) *Monitoring Poverty and Social Exclusion*. York: Joseph Rowntree Foundation

Ridge, T (2002) *Childhood Poverty and Social Exclusion: From a child's perspective*. Bristol: Policy Press

Shropshire, J and Middleton, S (1999) *Small Expectations: Learning to be poor?* York: York Publishing Services (for JRF)

Smaje, C (1995) *Health, 'Race' and Ethnicity: Making sense of the evidence*. London: King's Fund Institute

Wilkinson, RG (1996) *Unhealthy Societies – The afflictions of inequality*. London: Routledge

Employment 5

As with other chapters, it is difficult to consider the dimension of employment separate from the other dimensions on the 'missing' side of the triangle. This is well illustrated by the following quotation from a young woman living in a rural area of North Yorkshire:

'Before you can even look for a job ... you've got to know which areas you can get to easily so that you can be reliable. Before you get a house, you've got to get a job. So you've got to have money before you start, to get a car to get a job, or whatever.'
(Rugg and Jones, 1999)

This young woman demonstrates how employment is linked to *housing, income, and community resources* (lack of public transport) in rural areas.

This chapter begins with a consideration of the personal meanings of work and worklessness for different people. The links between employment and parenting capacity are then explored, before focusing on the way that employment can interact with other variables on the 'missing' side of the triangle, such as *social integration* and *family history*. There is then a consideration of the range of factors that contribute to structured disadvantages in employment opportunities, such as geographical location, race and disability. The chapter concludes with a summary of the employment-related issues that need to be taken into consideration in assessments of children in need and their families.

Personal meanings of work

Questions about the meaning of work elicit a wide range of responses. At the positive end of the spectrum there are responses such as *'It's the most important thing in my life', 'It defines who I am'*, and *'It gives me status and a purpose in my life.'* However, other people are likely to give more negative responses, such as *'It's just a job', 'It pays the bills'*, and *'It's the main cause of stress in my life and it will be the death of me.'*

This kind of reaction alerts us to the fact that employment can be a positive or a negative influence in people's lives or, perhaps more commonly, a complicated mixture of these two extremes. Besides the obvious potential material advantages of earning a regular wage or salary, paid employment also carries with it a number of latent functions, including structuring of personal time, status and identity, social interaction and participation in collective activities. These features of employment may be viewed positively or negatively, according to the fit between the needs of each individual, their social and economic circumstances and the particular characteristics of the work involved (Jahoda, 1981; 1982). How well does the content and nature of the work match the knowledge, skills and interests of the employee, and does it allow the individual concerned to exercise any control over what they do, and when, and how they do it?

Here we are entering the realm of social psychology, in which concepts such as locus of control (O'Brien, 1984; 1986; Fryer, 1986), learned helplessness (Seligman, 1975), attributions (Weiner, 1986) self-concepts (Kelvin and Jarrett, 1985) and self-efficacy (Bandura, 1986) can all be applied to increase our understanding of personal responses to employment and unemployment. A number of researchers have also applied models of stress and coping to issues of employment and unemployment. In the UK, Fineaman (1983) and Payne and Hartley (1987) found that stress resulting from unemployment could be understood in terms of the balance between the strengths and difficulties of the individual and their immediate and wider circumstances. In a similar way, Warr (1987) has identified a range of nine interrelated features of employment/unemployment that influence an individual's mental health, including their degree of personal control, opportunities for skill use, interpersonal interactions, status, and income. He made an analogy with the effects of vitamins on physical health, suggesting that mental health is dependent on a blend of these nine variables, with any significant deficiencies or overdoses, in one or more areas, likely to lead to problems.

In summary, then, both employment and unemployment carry with them different potential costs and benefits for different people in different situations. We should expect large variations in people's reactions to their work or lack of it and we should avoid making assumptions about the personal meanings that people attach to either employment or unemployment (Feather, 1990).

Employment and parenting capacity

Psychologists and sociologists have long been interested in the influences of employment on family life and parenting, coining such phrases as 'the long arm of the job' to describe this influence (Lynd and Lynd, 1929). Initially, this interest focused exclusively on the position of fathers (eg, Elder, 1974) but, with rising female employment outside the home, increasing attention has begun to be paid to mothers and dual-earner households (eg, Lerner and Galambos, 1986; Steinberg, 1986).

Work can influence parents' values and their views about what individual qualities are needed to succeed in the society in which they live. It also presents them with a range of different opportunities and constraints that affect their parenting capacity, including their physical and emotional availability and condition, as well as the skills, knowledge and personal relationships that arise out of their employment (Crouter and McHale, 1993). For example, Crouter (1984) found that the democratic culture of a particular manufacturing plant was transferred into the employees' parenting practices, as illustrated by the following statement from a divorced mother:

'I say things to my daughter that I know are the result of the way things are at work. I ask her 'What do you think about that?'...I tend to deal with her the way we deal with people at work. The logic is the same.' (quoted in Crouter and McHale, 1993, p183)

There is substantial research evidence about how different styles of parenting can influence children's development, fostering qualities such as independence and initiative (eg, Maccoby and Martin, 1983). There is also evidence of the way that work-induced stress can affect parental behaviour. For example, a small-scale study of air-traffic controllers by Repetti (1989) found fathers tended to be more socially and emotionally withdrawn following stressful days at work (cited in Crouter and McHale, 1993).

In recent years, much political attention has centred on the position of lone parents and their tendency, in the UK context, to be dependent on welfare benefits, rather than being actively involved in the labour market. Historically, benefit levels in the UK have been set at levels which leave the majority of lone-parent families living below the poverty line, with a whole range of negative consequences for parenting capacity and child development (see Chapter 4, Income, for details). The Labour government, elected in 1997, attempted to tackle this problem by increasing the financial support, the flexibility of work arrangements, and the childcare facilities available to lone parents in paid employment, as well as increasing benefit levels to non-working families with children. To date, these changes have had only a modest impact on most lone-parent families, with British parents still confronted by the historical legacy of very low levels of expensive daycare provision for their children. Nationally, it has been estimated that there is only one childcare place (either public or private) for every seven young children and only one after-school-club place for every fourteen children of school age (*Guardian*, 2001). A recent report has also revealed that British parents have the highest childcare bills in Europe, with the typical cost of a full-time nursery place for a 2-year-old being more than the average two-adults household spends on either housing or food (Daycare Trust, 2001). These problems, of scarce but expensive provision of daycare, are of importance to *all* poorer families with children, since government research reveals that *both* partners in workless families may need to obtain jobs in order to raise the family clear of poverty (Department of Social Security, 1999).

Although the government provides assistance to low-income working families in meeting the high costs of private daycare, through the Childcare Tax Credit, families still have to meet at least 30 per cent of the costs themselves, and non-working families do not qualify for this assistance at all. This would not be important if free local authority provision were plentiful but there are currently only about 20,000 such places accessible to the three million children living in workless families (Daycare Trust, 2001). Within the National Childcare Strategy, the government has set itself a target of providing a childcare place for every lone parent entering employment by March 2004, primarily through the creation of 45,000 new nursery places in 900 neighbourhood centres located in deprived areas. By the same date, they have also pledged to provide a nursery school place for all 3- and 4-year-olds whose parents want it. Unfortunately, despite these commitments, it is still likely that many parents who want to undertake paid work, or who are already doing so, will find themselves with personal circumstances, or living in geographical areas (particularly more rural locations), that continue to deny them access to appropriate daycare for their children.

Research into the effects on children's development in families where both parents are employed, or where a lone parent is employed, is notoriously influenced by the assumptions and values of those funding, undertaking or publicising the research. There is often an unhelpful focus on maternal employment and a tendency to equate this with potentially harmful effects on young children's development. However, more objective assessments of the effects of daycare on the development of young children identifies the quality of the daycare provided as the crucial factor. A child receiving a better standard of care, with a childminder or in a nursery, than they receive at home, is likely to benefit developmentally, whilst a poorer standard of care than that provided at home is likely to result in some developmental disadvantages (Moss and Melhuish, 1991).

As already discussed, the effects of both work and worklessness on children's development is also likely to be influenced by the personal meaning attached to work by parents, and the environmental context of the family. A parent who wants to go out to work, for personal fulfilment as well as for financial gain, and who enjoys their work, is in a vastly different position from another parent who feels coerced into working, because of financial pressures, and who can only find work which is profoundly unsatisfying. The same is true of not going out to work – it is the personal, familial, and circumstantial contexts within which this occurs that are likely to be significant when trying to assess the impact that it has on parenting capacity and child development. One of the most important contextual factors influencing parenting and child development is the parent's social networks (Jack, 2000) and it is the links between these networks and employment that we now consider.

Social networks and employment

The interrelationship between adult *social integration* and employment provides a clear and powerful illustration of the ecological principles upon which the Assessment Framework for children in need is based (Department of Health, 2000). As we will go on to illustrate, these two factors help to mutually reinforce one another, with social networks providing a pathway to employment, and employment, in turn, helping to extend personal social networks.

Of direct relevance to workers involved in assessments will be the way that disadvantages in *employment* opportunities, *community resources*, and *social integration* may have an impact on an individual's capacity to provide parenting in a way that is regarded as appropriate. This is illustrated by the following case example.

> Mary Stones is a lone parent with an 8-year-old child, Jason. She has no formal work skills and lives on a large estate where there are few unskilled work opportunities. The only employment available is early-morning or evening cleaning work in the city centre. Mary has a very limited social network on the estate, and there are no suitable childcare facilities available locally. Desperate to find work that gets her out of her flat, Mary takes an early-morning cleaning job. She has no one to ask to look after Jason when she leaves early in the morning to take the firm's minibus into the city centre. She leaves breakfast ready for Jason and he is expected to lock up the flat and walk to school. After only a short time, a neighbour contacts social services to report that she is worried that Jason is being left alone.

Fischer (1982), a North American sociologist, was one of the first researchers to provide empirical evidence of the relationship between employment and personal social networks of relationships. He interviewed a community sample of over 1,000 people, in town and city locations, in the San Francisco area of the United States. He found that higher levels of education and income, and being in employment, were all associated with more extensive and supportive friendship networks. Subsequent research has confirmed these findings in different cultural contexts, with one review concluding that: '.... to a significant degree, a parent's network reflects his or her position in the social structure of a given society.' (Cochran, 1993, p149).

Individuals are increasingly likely to make friends and to meet their partners through work, at a time when other social trends appear to be leading to increasing fragmentation of personal relationships. This is illustrated in a recent survey of employees, by the career consultants Sanders and Sydney, in which 70 per cent of men and 90 per cent of women said they had made important friendships through their work, and 25 per cent of respondents had met their life partner at work. Nearly three-quarters of those questioned said they had experienced a sense of personal loss when leaving a job (*Guardian*, 2000).

The two-way nature of this relationship, between *social integration* and employment, is demonstrated by research that shows how important social networks can be in finding employment. For example, research for the Joseph Rowntree Foundation, into the social exclusion of young adults in Scotland, revealed that social networks were the key to securing work, with a lack of network members representing an important barrier to employment (Pavis, Platt and Hubbard, 2000; Cartmel and Furlong, 2000).

In similar vein, a recent pamphlet produced by the think-tank Demos highlighted the futility of most government-inspired attempts to improve the job-seeking prospects of unemployed people, by bringing them together in 'job-clubs'. As one frustrated member of such a club in Liverpool (who was being instructed in how to write job application letters) stated:

'The way you get work around here is to put the word around your mates, your old man's mates, around the pub. Sending letters blind is a bloody waste of time.'
(Perri, 1997)

The conclusion of this piece of work was that the best way to find work is to utilise a diverse network of relationships with people already in employment, rather than relying on instructing groups of unemployed people together. This conclusion is supported by research in the United States, where a lack of social ties was found to present a structural barrier to joining the labour market, especially for certain minority ethnic groups with lower levels of education. Social networks, containing weak ties with a higher proportion of employed members, on the other hand, provided increased access to employment (Reingold, 1999). Of course, the roots of these differences in social networks can often be traced to childhood experiences and circumstances, as can a wide range of other factors that significantly influence employment prospects in adult life. This is the area that we will now go on to explore.

The influence of childhood characteristics and experiences on future employment

Chapter 4 on *income* draws attention to the powerful links between a child's future earning potential as an adult and the earnings of their parents and grandparents (HM Treasury, 1999). This Treasury document also highlights the close correlation between poor achievement at school and the risk of unemployment. For example, the rate of unemployment for people with no academic qualifications in 1997 was double that of those with five A–C grade GCSEs (*Guardian*, 1999).

An in-depth study of 98 young people aged 15–25 years, living in a disadvantaged neighbourhood in the North East of England demonstrates clearly the way that personal characteristics and experiences in childhood (often linked to *family history and functioning*) in interaction with the wider environment, serve to shape later opportunities in adult life (Johnston et al, 2000). Unemployment, in the study area, was estimated to be about 40 per cent, with employment opportunities for young adults being particularly limited. The area had become notorious for high levels of crime, much of which was drug-related. The researchers found that childhood experiences, such as family bereavement or disruption, and disengagement from formal education and training were crucial to later experiences of drug use, crime and unemployment. However, they also found that positive life events and relationships with significant adults outside the family could successfully divert young people away from these negative pathways.

Research evidence from the USA serves to confirm the way that family economic conditions in early childhood have a significant influence on subsequent educational achievement and employment (Duncan et al, 1998). A significant proportion of these effects appear to be due to the relationship between *income* and the quality of the home environment, in terms of opportunities for learning, parent–child interactions, physical conditions and parental conflict (Smith, Brooks-Gunn and Klebanov, 1997; Conger, Conger and Elder, 1997). Other studies have shown that a constellation of family factors, reaching back into early childhood – low IQ, poor reading skills, lack of qualifications, low income, single-parent family, anti-social behaviour, and family conflict – significantly increase the risk of later unemployment (Caspi et al, 1998).

It can therefore be seen that *family history and functioning*, as well as certain personal and environmental characteristics, begin to shape later employment prospects from an early age. These findings, from both sides of the Atlantic, have been important in the UK government's thinking about improving the readiness of young children, from disadvantaged circumstances, for education. The main planks of social policy in this area, besides the objective of reducing child poverty (see Chapter 4 on income), are the establishment of the Sure Start programme for pre-school children and their families, and a range of measures designed to improve the educational achievement of all children. Although evaluation of all of these initiatives is ongoing, their combined effectiveness, in terms of employment, will only become evident when the young children currently benefiting from them progress through the education system and on to their adult lives.

Structured disadvantages and employment (location, gender, race and disability)

This section concerns the way in which different groups of people experience particular disadvantages in employment because of the way that society is structured and arranged.

The first issue concerns where people live. Wide variations in rates of unemployment in different areas of the UK make it obvious that whether or not an individual can find and maintain employment is strongly influenced by where they live. Over the years there has rightly been a great deal of concern about the effects of the large-scale restructuring of traditional manufacturing industries on different communities. In the face of a widespread economic recession, and the 'free-market' policies of successive Conservative governments during the 1980s, unemployment rose dramatically, leaving many working-class communities, predominantly in the Midlands and the North of England, the South of Wales and the lowland conurbations of Scotland, without any short- or medium-term prospects of economic recovery. Social welfare staff working in these areas do not need anyone to tell them how devastating these changes have been for the lives of hundreds of thousands of families and children, as well as the communities within which they live, many of which have been damaged almost beyond repair. Since the 1980s, successive governments in the UK have devoted large sums of money to the creation of new employment and economic regeneration of the worst-hit areas. In addition, the major problems experienced in more rural areas, as a result of the BSE and foot and mouth crises, amongst other pressures, have begun to attract research interest and government attention.

The Joseph Rowntree Foundation, for example, has supported a number of research projects looking at the challenges facing people living in rural locations. In one of these projects, researchers at the University of Aberdeen conducted an ethnographic study of 52 two-parent households with at least one working adult and one child under 13 years of age, in three different rural locations. Most of the men were in continuous, although often insecure, full-time employment (often involving multiple jobs). They took for granted the role of economic provider for their families and often worked flexible hours allowing them to accommodate family commitments and to play an active role in parenting tasks. By contrast, the employment histories of the women in the study tended to be fragmented, reflecting their more central role in running the family home and caring for their children. Their employment patterns were a response to changing family circumstances, including their partner's work, the age of their children, the financial pressures on the family and the availability of childcare. Many chose not to take on paid work, especially when their children were younger, but those that did so tended to work only part-time and valued not only the extra income but also the personal and social rewards it provided. Those women who undertook full-time work, usually out of financial necessity, found that it involved a degree of role strain, preventing them from being involved in the parental role as much as they would have wished (Mauthner, McKee and Strell, 2001).

In another study of a random sample of sixty 22-year-olds living in rural areas of North Yorkshire (Rugg and Jones, 1999), issues of employment, housing and community resources presented challenges to their ability to establish their own households and families, independent of their own parents. Even dual-income couples in these rural locations found it difficult to afford to rent or buy a home of their own at this age. Most young people in this study were in employment but their work tended to be low paid, with limited prospects for career development. For those who had gone to university, finding graduate-status employment almost inevitably involved them in leaving their home area to seek work in more urban locations.

The government has responded to this growing awareness of the difficulties faced by rural communities by publishing a rural White Paper, setting out plans for revitalising rural economies and increasing employment opportunities, and by establishing the Countryside Agency. However, to date these proposals are largely aspirational and set within a very general framework, not yet providing the sort of detailed plans required to solve the problems of, for example, workless parents wishing to move into employment. Lack of community resources, in the form of transport and accessible and affordable childcare, is a major problem for people living in rural locations, with a recent report estimating that 96 per cent of rural parishes lack any public nursery provision (NCH, 2001).

Another major cause of structural inequalities in employment is race, with surveys consistently revealing higher levels of unemployment among certain minority ethnic groups. For example, a survey undertaken by the Policy Studies Institute (PSI, 1997) found that all minority ethnic groups, except men and women of Chinese descent, experienced higher levels of unemployment than the white population, with Caribbean, Pakistani and Bangladeshi groups being the most disadvantaged. These findings are confirmed by another study, using receipt of Housing and Council Tax Benefits as a measure of low income. Once again, the same three minority ethnic groups were found to be the most disadvantaged (Platt and Noble, 1999). Part of the explanation for these findings can be found in the geographical locations of different minority ethnic communities. More than half of African-Caribbeans and Africans, and over a third of South Asians, live in areas with the highest levels of unemployment. Only one in twenty of these groups live in low unemployment areas, compared to one in five of the white population (Chahal, 2000). Once again, we see the way that different factors interact with one another (in this case ethnic background and geographical location) to reinforce disadvantages and inequalities.

This tendency for various factors to interact with each other in ways that strengthen disadvantages is further illustrated by the final example in this chapter, concerning families with one or more disabled members, either adults or children. Parents of disabled children experience restrictions on both their employment opportunities and their earning potential when in work (Jack and Jack, 2000). For example, very few mothers with a disabled child work outside the home – only one in fifty, according to a recent survey, compared to nearly one in four of the general population of mothers with children (Marchant and Jones, 2000). Black and minority ethnic families of children with disabilities are likely to be particularly disadvantaged, due to the higher levels of unemployment that these ethnic groups experience, as already discussed. Similar disadvantages in employment are also experienced by families in which one or both of the parents suffers from either a chronic illness or a disability, as evidenced by a recent government report into the inadequate support services currently provided by health and local authorities for these parents (SSI, 2000).

Issues for assessment

The evidence summarised in this chapter has made it clear that employment and unemployment, or working and not working, mean very different things to different people, depending on a wide range of individual, family and environmental factors.

To begin with, child welfare workers need to be aware of the importance of the personal meanings attached to either working or not working by different family members. Specifically, in relation to parenting capacity and the development of children, workers need to understand the impact of such meanings on parents' self-esteem and identity. For example, the quality of the emotional warmth that a parent is able to provide, which will affect the child's emotional and behavioural development, is going to be linked to their own sense of well-being. Assessments with parents should therefore explore their views about employment-related issues, including their aspirations for the future, and their perceptions about the way that these issues are impacting on their parenting. Similarly, workers should be aware of the meaning that children attach to their parents' or carers' employment, which is likely to have an impact on the child's own sense of identity.

Beyond the effects of employment-related issues on individual psychology, there are a number of important ways in which they can have a major influence on family life, for all family members. One of the most obvious of these influences on parenting was illustrated by one of the case examples referred to in the text above (p76). Mary Stones' hours of work, combined with a lack of *community resources* (affordable local childcare), *social integration* and *wider family* support, took her away from the parenting role at the beginning of the day, leading to allegations of neglect. For other parents the location, hours of work, or nature of their employment may either help to facilitate their parenting, or be a source of considerable pressure. Assessments will therefore need to establish whether parental employment provides, for example, essential income for the family, or regular or extended absences from the family home, or is the source of either important social network members or damaging levels of stress for parents. These matters may have significant implications for their ability to provide such things as emotional warmth, safety, and guidance for their children. In turn, these aspects of parenting capacity are likely to influence various aspects of children's development, including their health, education, emotional and behavioural development, and family and social relationships. Again, the best way of approaching these issues is to talk directly to different family members about their own perceptions of the way that they are affecting the family. Helping parents and children to clarify and share their thoughts and feelings about the effects of employment-related issues on one another, and the links that these issues have with their wider family and environmental circumstances, is likely to be an important element in the assessment of many families of children in need.

As part of this area of assessment, workers will also be exploring the background to parents' employability in their early experience and *family history*. We have already noted the strong associations between early educational and family experiences and employment and earnings in adult life (Caspi *et al*, 1998). It appears that low parental income has its greatest influence on child development through its effects on the quality of the home environment, in terms of opportunities for learning, parent–child interactions, physical conditions and levels of parental conflict (Smith, Brooks-Gunn and Klebanov, 1997; Conger, Conger and Elder, 1997). It is therefore crucial that assessments of children in need are used to identify the harmful factors that exist in their home environments and to provide the information upon which to develop interventions that will enhance these environments. The task here will involve constructing a framework in which the strengths and pressures, arising from the interplay between individual characteristics and wider environmental circumstances, can be assessed in order to highlight the main areas for supportive or therapeutic interventions. For example, for parents who are unemployed and wish to gain work, are there any areas of skill and knowledge that could be developed, through education and training, to improve a parent's employability? Are there any ways in which the parent's social support networks, or the community resources available to them, could be enhanced in ways that would increase their chances of gaining or maintaining employment? Assessments will also need to consider some of the factors behind structural inequalities in employment. For example, what are the implications of the family's geographical location, or ethnic background, and do either the parent(s) or any of the children suffer from a chronic illness or disability that has implications for the parent's employment or earning potential? Whilst workers may not have direct access to the resources needed to provide solutions to some of the issues identified, including them in assessments is likely to be empowering to family members. They should also help to identify other agencies whose decisions and policies need to be influenced, on behalf of either individuals or particular vulnerable groups.

References

Bandura, A (1986) *Social Foundations of Thought and Action: A social cognitive theory*. Englewood Cliffs, NJ: Prentice-Hall

Cartmel, F and Furlong, A (2000) *Youth Unemployment in Rural Areas*. York: York Publishing Services

Caspi, A, Moffitt, TE, Entner Wright, BR, Silva, PA (1998) Early failure in the labour market: childhood and adolescent predictors of unemployment in the transition to adulthood. *American Sociological Review*, **63**, 424–51

Chahal, K (2000) *Ethnic Diversity, Neighbourhoods and Housing*. York: Joseph Rowntree Foundation

Cochran, M (1993) Parenting and personal social networks. In T Luster and L Okagaki (eds) *Parenting: An ecological perspective*, pp149–78. Hillsdale, NJ: Lawrence Erlbaum Associates

Conger, R, Conger, K, Elder, G (1997) Family economic hardship and adolescent adjustment: mediating and moderating processes. In G Duncan and J Brooks-Gunn (eds) *Consequences of Growing Up Poor*, pp288–310. New York: Russell Sage

Crouter, AC (1984) Participative work as an influence on human development. *Journal of Applied Developmental Psychology*, **5**, 71–90

Crouter, AC and McHale, SM (1993) The long arm of the job: influences of parental work on childrearing. In: T Luster and L Okagaki (eds) *Parenting: An Ecological Perspective*, pp179–202. Hillside, NJ: Lawrence Erlbaum Associates

Daycare Trust (2001) *The Price Parents Pay*. London: Daycare Trust

Department of Health (2000) *Framework for the Assessment of Children in Need and their Families*. London: The Stationery Office

Department of Social Security (1999) *Parents and Employment* (Research Report No.107), Leeds: Corporate Document Services

Duncan, GJ, Brooks-Gunn, J, Yeung, WJ, Smith, JR (1998) How much does childhood poverty affect the life chances of children? *American Sociological Review*, **63**, 406–23

Elder, GH, Jnr (1974) *Children of the Great Depression*. Chicago: University of Chicago Press

Feather, NT (1990) *The Psychological Impact of Unemployment*. New York: Springer-Verlag

Fineaman, S (1983) *White Collar Unemployment: Impact and stress*. Chichester: Wiley

Fischer, C (1982) *To Dwell among Friends: Personal networks in town and city*. Chicago: University of Chicago Press

Fryer, D (1986) Employment deprivation and personal agency during employment: a critical discussion of Jahoda's explanation of the psychological effects of unemployment. *Social Behaviour*, 1,3-23

Guardian (1999) *40pc of children born poor*. 29 March, p7

Guardian (2000) *People 'rely on friends at work'*. 12 October, p11

Guardian (2001) *Analysis*. 25 July, p17

HM Treasury (1999) *Tackling Poverty and Extending Opportunity*. London: The Stationery Office

Jack, G (2000) Ecological influences on parenting and child development. *British Journal of Social Work*, **30**, 703-20

Jack, G and Jack, D (2000) Ecological social work: the application of a systems model of development in context. In P Stepney and D Ford (eds) *Social Work Models, Methods and Theories: A framework for practice.* pp93–104. Lyme Regis: Russell House Publishing

Jahoda, M (1981) Work, employment and unemployment: values, theories and approaches in social research. *American Psychologist,* **36**, 184–91

Jahoda, M (1982) *Employment and Unemployment: A social-psychological analysis.* Cambridge: Cambridge University Press

Johnston, L, MacDonald, R, Mason, P, Ridley, L, Webster, C (2000) *Snakes and Ladders: Young people, transitions and social exclusion.* London: The Policy Press

Kelvin, P and Jarrett, JE (1985) *Unemployment: Its social psychological effects.* Cambridge: Cambridge University Press

Lerner, JV and Galambos, NL (1986), Child development and family change: the influences of maternal employment on infants and toddlers. In LP Lipsitt and C Rovee-Collier (eds) *Advances in Infancy Research* (Vol IV) pp39–86. Norwood. NJ: Ablex

Lynd, RS and Lynd, HM (1929) *Middletown: A study in modern American culture.* New York: Harcourt, Brace and World

Maccoby, E and Martin, J (1983) Socialization in the context of the family: parent-child interaction. In PH Mussen (ed) *Handbook of Child Psychology* (Vol IV), pp39–86. New York: Wiley

Marchant, R and Jones, M (2000) Assessing the needs of disabled children and their families. In Department of Health *Assessing Children in Need and their Families: Practice guidance,* pp73–112. London: The Stationery Office

Mauthner, N, McKee, L, Strell, M (2001) *Work and Family Life in Rural Communities.* York: York Publishing Services

Moss, P and Melhuish, E (eds) (1991) *Current Issues in Day Care for Young Children.* London: HMSO

National Children's Home (2001) *Challenging the Rural Idyll.* London: NCH

O'Brien, GE (1984) Locus on control, work and retirement. In HM Lefcourt (ed) *Research with the Locus of Control Construct* (Vol 3), pp7–72. New York: Academic Press

O'Brien, GE (1986) *Psychology of Work and Unemployment.* Chichester: Wiley

Pavis, S, Platt, S, Hubbard, G (2000) *Young People in Rural Scotland: Pathways to social inclusion and exclusion.* York: York Publishing Services

Payne, RL and Hartley, J (1987) A test of a model for explaining the affective experience of unemployed men. *Journal of Occupational Psychology,* **60**, 31–47

Perri 6 (1997) *Escaping Poverty: From safety nets to networks of opportunity.* London: Demos

Platt, L and Noble, M (1999) *Race, Place and Poverty: Ethnic groups and low income distributions* (York: Joseph Rowntree Foundation)

Policy Studies Institute (1997) *The Fourth National Survey of Ethnic Minorities in Britain: Diversity and disadvantage*. London: PSI

Reingold, DA (1999) Social networks and the employment problem of the urban poor. *Urban Studies*, **36**(11), 1907–32

Repetti, R (1989) *Daily job stress and father–child interaction*, Paper presented at the biennial meeting of the Society for Research in Child Development, Kansas City, MO

Rugg, J and Jones, A (1999) *Getting a Job, Finding a Home: Rural youth transitions*. W. Sussex: Biblios Publishers

Seligman, MEP (1975) *Helplessness: On depression, development and death*. San Francisco: Freeman

Smith, J, Brooks-Gunn, J, Klebanov, P (1997) Consequences of growing up poor for young children. In G Duncan and J Brooks-Gunn (eds) *Consequences of Growing up Poor*. New York: Russell Sage

Social Services Inspectorate (2000) *A Jigsaw of Services*. London: Department of Health

Steinberg, L (1986) Latchkey children and susceptibility to peer pressure: an ecological analysis. *Developmental Psychology*, **22**, 433–39

Warr, PB (1987) *Work, Unemployment and Mental Health*. Oxford: Clarendon Press

Weiner, B (1986) *An Attributional Theory of Motivation and Emotion*. New York: Springer-Verlag

Housing 6

The Department of Health's Children in Need census (Department of Health, 2000a) does not identify housing as a separate category for social services involvement with children in need and their families. Adverse housing conditions and homelessness are subsumed within the much broader category of 'Family in acute stress', making it impossible to disentangle housing issues from a whole range of other problems that are responsible for a child being designated as 'in need'.

The very low profile of housing issues has been a serious omission in relation to assessments with children and their families, since many of the difficulties faced by families that come into contact with welfare agencies are linked, in one way or another, to their housing circumstances. According to the government's own figures, as many as 3 million households were living in poor housing in 2002. As the housing charity, Shelter, has pointed out: 'Government programmes to tackle poverty and social exclusion will not deliver for them until their housing needs are met' (Shelter, 2002a, p1).

There has been a lack of research in the UK into the impact of housing on the welfare of parents and children. Although, in recent years, there has been some important work carried out into the effects of homelessness on children (see below), this has not been matched by more general work on the relationship between housing and child development or parenting capacity. Without guidance from a body of relevant UK research, the level of analysis of this relationship has inevitably been weak, and the extent to which it has been incorporated into assessments with children and their families has been very limited.

This lack of attention to the effects of housing on family functioning often runs counter to the perspective of families on their difficulties. Our experience has been that, in some circumstances, social workers have either overlooked or discounted the importance of housing, even when the family in question sees it as important. This may be because professional workers perceive that housing conditions are beyond their sphere of influence and responsibility, or because their training and their employers' procedures, structured by government requirements and targets, mean that they focus on issues within the family, instead of making an ecological assessment of the way that the internal world of the family interacts with their external surroundings.

This difference in the significance attached to housing and location by workers and families was illustrated some years ago by Packman and her colleagues (Packman, Randall and Jacques, 1986). Their study of children at risk of reception into care in two local authorities provides useful information about the role of housing in social work decision-making. In their sample of 361 children, one in seven lived in dwellings assessed by social workers as being in a poor state, and slightly more of them were without any outdoor space of their own. The group of children who were admitted to care via court orders during the study period, because of their family circumstances and experiences, were the most likely to come from families living in poor-standard accommodation. However, whilst only 14 per cent of the overall sample were judged by social workers to be living in poor housing, nearly a quarter (23 per cent) of the parents interviewed were unhappy with their accommodation and a slightly higher proportion of them (28 per cent) disliked the neighbourhoods in which they lived. Packman and colleagues concluded that where people lived affected all aspects of their lives, and the problems associated with either their accommodation or its location were often seemingly of much greater importance to them than was acknowledged by their social workers.

There are many interconnections between housing and the other domains on this side of the assessment triangle. For example, housing and location will have an impact on *social integration* and the family's access to *community resources*. At a more general level, the quality, safety, and appropriateness of housing provision will all have connections with the *income* of families (Morris and Winn, 1990). Amongst home-owners, there is a strong relationship between property value and social class. Certain disadvantaged groups, such as lone parents, minority ethnic families, and low-income earners, are more likely to be living in lower-value properties which are also likely to be in the worst condition (Forrest and Murie, 1995). The ability of parents to influence the environment in which they live is likely to have wider implications for themselves and their families. In terms of their sense of competence as adults, as well as their ability to impart appropriate values to their children and provide them with adequate levels of protection as they are growing up, the sense of powerlessness experienced by parents living in poor housing on low incomes is likely to have a major impact.

General housing pressures

Housing provides a clear illustration of the processes that underpin the ecological model. Poor housing can be seen to be both a consequence of social exclusion and one of its principal causes. This means that solutions to housing problems are rarely to be found in bricks and mortar alone. Action is also likely to be needed, simultaneously, in relation to all of the other factors associated with social exclusion, such as health, education, leisure, and transport services, as well as training and employment opportunities (Lee and Murie, 1997).

In terms of understanding the impact of housing provision on the most vulnerable children, the process of 'residualisation' is important. Analysis of the changing characteristics of social housing areas in the latter half of the twentieth century show that this process greatly affected the social composition of a large number of areas (Malpass, 1990; Burrows, 1999). Residualisation refers to the process whereby social housing has increasingly been used to accommodate disadvantaged groups. As a result, areas of social housing have come to be increasingly distinguished from other, more favoured areas. There is an increasing concentration of people on very low incomes in rented accommodation and a virtual absence of people on middle or high incomes.

Nearly three-quarters of tenants in the social rented sector now come from the poorest 40 per cent of the population (Hills, 2001). In general, the size, quality and location of housing that consumers can obtain depends on their ability to pay (Malpass and Murie, 1999). Whilst the UK still has an extensive system of state intervention in the housing market, including the provision of subsidised housing and Housing Benefit payments, that directly affect more than a quarter of the population, the way in which this operates often tends to reinforce, rather than counteract, processes of social and economic polarisation.

One key characteristic associated with residualisation is that social housing areas now include a disproportionate number of elderly people and low-income families with young children. This applies not only to local authority housing, but also to property controlled by housing associations. For instance, research on tenant participation in housing association areas found that high child density was a key issue (Kemp and Fordham, 1997).

Race and housing

One particularly important aspect of residualisation is the significant role of racial background. The ways in which housing is allocated, and the housing 'choice' of black and other minority ethnic groups, may have a cumulative impact on lack of access to housing resources (Somerville and Steele, 2002). One aspect of this is that different ethnic groups tend to have different housing tenures and types. For instance, in one study it was found that Caribbean, Chinese and Bangladeshi households were the most likely to occupy flats. Nearly 40 per cent of households in these groups occupied this type of accommodation, compared with 16 per cent of white, 13 per cent of Indian and African Asian, and just 7 per cent of Pakistani households (Lakey, 1997, p207). Lakey also noted that a fifth of Bangladeshi flat-dwellers actually lived above the third floor, compared with just over one in ten Caribbean flat-dwellers and well under one in twenty from other ethnic groups.

Also, although Asian and Pakistani families are more likely to be owner-occupiers, this is not necessarily consistent with their being in better quality accommodation. This is illustrated in one study that found '... owner-occupiers of Indian/African, Asian, Pakistani and Bangladeshi origin were three or four times as likely as social tenants or white or Caribbean owners to lack ... basic amenities.' (Modood and Berthoud, 1997, p209). They also found generally lower levels of housing satisfaction among minority ethnic groups than among white groups.

Housing, physical safety and illness

There is much evidence about the extent of accidents and illnesses that children experience in the home. Approximately a million children a year go to hospital as a result of accidents in the home (Royal Society for the Prevention of Accidents, 1998). Within the home, there will therefore be issues for assessment in terms of safety. These will include such items as worn carpeting or rough flooring, which can be dangerous for children, furniture placed near windows when there are young children in the family, and kitchen safety issues, including faulty cooking appliances and the safety and position of kettles and other electrical appliances. It is the responsibility of those involved in assessments of children in need and their families to ascertain the safety of accommodation in relation to the child's needs and stage of development.

There are, once again, important links here to household income. Very low household income may mean that compromises have to be made in terms of safety. The purchase of equipment such as stair gates, the replacement of faulty electrical goods, and other everyday safety expenses, can all place major financial burdens on families surviving on low incomes. These issues may be a particular problem for households dependent on income support, especially in the context of Social Fund rules, limiting most assistance to loans rather than grants. There will also be many other safety issues in relation to family accommodation, concerning external as well as internal safety. Windows and balconies will, for instance, be particularly important in this respect, as illustrated by the following case example.

> In a block of flats the balconies had 'protective' mesh on them. Many of the parents were anxious about this and felt the mesh could be used by small children to climb over the balcony, and did not allow their children onto the balconies.

Poor housing also affects the health of children and their parents, although it has often been difficult to separate the effects of housing problems from the effects of other disadvantages experienced by those who live in poor housing (Blackburn, 1991). However, some studies have managed to overcome these difficulties, by controlling for different variables. One such study demonstrated a clear association between damp home conditions and increased levels of respiratory and other complaints in both children and adults. These associations remained significant even after controlling for other indicators of socio-economic disadvantage, such as income, unemployment and overcrowding, as well as behavioural influences, such as smoking (Platt *et al*, 1989). Overcrowding is, of course, a housing problem in its own right, that has been shown to be associated with a range of physical and mental health difficulties, such as increased levels of depression (Brown and Harris, 1978).

The psycho-social processes that accompany material deprivation, such as poor housing, will be particularly important for welfare professionals to understand when undertaking assessments (Wilkinson, 1999). Without an appreciation of the interactions between socio-economic circumstances and psycho-social health, there is a danger that parents will be blamed for behaviour that is primarily a response to their wider environmental circumstances. In a similar way, a failure to fully understand the risks posed by dangerous environments, over which parents living in poor housing and dangerous neighbourhoods may have very limited control, can lead to assessments that erroneously suggest that parental neglect is an issue.

This is a particular danger of the Home Conditions Scale, provided by the Department of Health to accompany the Framework for Assessment of Children in Need and their Families (Department of Health, 2000b). This is, essentially, an instrument for gauging the cleanliness of the home environment, with high scores having been shown to be correlated with deficits in children's language and intellectual development (Davie *et al.* 1984). Whilst the accompanying guidance warns against using it in isolation from other sources of information in assessments, there is no discussion of the sort of difficulties and pressures experienced by families that may give rise to poor standards of cleanliness and hygiene in the home. Furthermore, the guidance suggests it is 'best used as a mental checklist' and that 'it will usually be unhelpful to share…with the caregiver'. It goes on to state that such openness 'could upset the establishment of partnership – a good working relationship is of overriding importance.' (Department of Health, 2000b p24).

In our view, workers who approach their task with a proper understanding of the overall ecology of families will be in a position to convey, to the parents and children with whom they are working, an awareness of the difficulties they are experiencing and the full range of interacting factors that are likely to be at the root of those difficulties. The development and discussion of these shared understandings is surely the basis for real partnership working, rather than the formulation of private judgements that cannot be openly discussed with parents and children.

Housing and proximity

The physical location of accommodation for families can determine whether there is immediate local support and security for families, or whether families are locked into neighbourhoods that are characterised by conflict and risk. The dangers posed by particular locations, in terms of offending and drug-taking, for example, are well known to welfare professionals working in those areas. However, there are many other locations, that pose serious risks to children and families, that can go unrecognised.

This has been graphically illustrated for us recently by some work undertaken by one of our research students in a small town. Following awareness, in the local primary school, of a high incidence of sexualised behaviour by a number of its pupils, it was discovered that these children were all living in the same area of the town. This consisted of a cul-de-sac of 40 dwellings, one of which, it subsequently turned out, was occupied by two convicted sex offenders. One of these offenders was using his employment at the local newsagents to gain access to children for the purposes of sexual abuse.

Of the other dwellings, 15 were occupied by families about whom there were present or recent child protection concerns, or more general welfare concerns, of one kind or another. However, because of the individual way that referrals had been made, over a period of time, and the fact that several agencies were involved with the different families, none of the professionals involved was aware of the overall picture.

A combination of the local housing department's allocation policies and a failure of the welfare agencies involved to effectively share information that identified the geographical concentration of problems in one small area led to the creation of a very high-risk environment that would have made safe parenting a severe challenge to any family living there.

In some of the more hard-pressed communities, in different parts of the country, where there are disadvantages associated with a combination of housing problems, *income* and *community resources*, there can also be very significant difficulties between neighbours. Unpopular housing may lead to high rates of mobility and transience and a lack of social cohesion. This will often reveal itself in tensions between neighbours. Two examples can be used to illustrate this.

> The G family live in a cul-de-sac on a large housing estate. The pressures and demands that the family experience have been made considerably more extreme because the family are being scapegoated by local neighbours and their children. There has been taunting of the children and the parents when they go outside the house and on several occasions rubbish has been thrown onto the front doorstep of the house. When asked to talk about their problems the parents attribute a lot of their difficulties to the behaviour of local children and adults and the pressures and insecurities it puts on them. They see one solution to their difficulties as being a move away from their street. They are particularly keen to move to another street, only a little way away, where they have other family members living and where they would be accepted and supported.

The missing side of the triangle

Difficult physical proximity to other households is also illustrated by this case description from a market town, which also indicates the way that the layout and development of housing can pose particular problems for families.

> Sarah England is a lone parent who lives in a small block of flats in a medium-sized market town. Half of the flats are one-bedroom flats and half are two-bedroom flats. The two-bedroom flats are allocated to young families, whereas the single-bedroom flats are occupied by people on their own. One consequence of this pattern of accommodation is that families are typically living side by side with single men. Sarah experiences real difficulties in this situation. There are problems about noise late at night and issues around drug taking and drug dealing. Her flat door-bell is constantly ringing, even in the middle of the night. This creates pressures and insecurity for Sarah and also fear and insecurity for the children.

Who the family lives alongside is also likely to produce particular issues for black, other minority ethnic and dual-heritage children. It can have implications for their developing sense of identity and, in extreme cases, it may have implications for their physical security. The following case example illustrates this.

> Mary is a white lone parent who lives in a street of walk-up flats on a predominantly white estate. She has two dual-heritage children, aged 5 and 6. Over the months there have been increasing incidents of racial abuse directed at the children. Often these have been from people living nearby. Mary feels that a move, only a short distance away, would be a solution to the family's victimisation. She says there is a street, only three or four streets away, where she would get support and where there are more racially mixed households.

Once again, we can see that the family's preferred solution to their difficulties is a very local move of house. Unfortunately, in our experience, staff responsible for arranging social housing transfers very often overlook the importance of maintaining local support systems, and offer alternative accommodation on different estates, or on the other side of the town or city.

Housing and networks

The provision of housing and its location will have an impact on the social networks that children and parents develop. There are, therefore, clear links between housing provision and the social integration of families. While the housing of some families will support and strengthen their networks, with accommodation in areas close to their family and friends, the opposite will be the case for many families, whose accommodation separates them from important sources of support.

Also, the family's accommodation will have particular implications for their children's networks, which are likely to be highly localised, particularly in more disadvantaged areas, where a smaller proportion of families have their own transport. Who children live alongside, who they walk to school with, and who they play with, will all have significance for their development.

There may also be some significant interactions between a parent's perception of the neighbourhood and the characteristics of a child's social networks. The following case example shows the way in which this may have negative implications for children's friendships.

> The James family lived in a two-bedroom flat on the first floor of a block of walk-up flats. The flats had a high incidence of break-ins. Mr James told the family centre worker that he did not allow his 7-year-old son to have friends back into his house. He said the reason for this was that he was worried that the children would see his stereo equipment and tell their parents who would then break in to steal it.

Housing and financial pressues

Although many families that workers come into contact with will be in receipt of Housing Benefit covering their rent, many families will face financial difficulties as a result of their housing circumstances.

For families dependent on income support, for example, setting up or moving home will often involve taking out loans that produce pressures on family finances. Some families will take on very high levels of debt, through involvement with catalogue and loan companies, whilst others will take out loans through the Social Fund. Although there may be some limited grant availability for essential items, through the Social Fund, the likelihood is that families will have to take out loans. At the present time, there is pressure being put on the government to increase the grant element of the Social Fund, but currently most families have to take out loans which mean, in effect, that they have to live below the income support level.

For some families, the fear of the Social Fund, and indebtedness in general, will mean that they are not prepared to take out loans. No matter how great their needs, they prefer to manage somehow, in what may be very poor quality or even dangerous surroundings, that significantly compromise their ability to parent successfully. This is the lesser of two evils for some families. We also know that poverty and low income affect certain groups more than others. One of the most hard-pressed groups in British society are young single mothers. The particular difficulties faced by this group, in setting up their own homes, have been highlighted by Speak (1995), who found that their families could often afford to offer only very limited assistance. She also found that staying in the family home, while awaiting rehousing, could strain relationships so that even less family support was available when the move occurred. Speak also found that furnishing a home, even to a basic standard, meant that young single mothers had to take out loans which they found costly and difficult to repay.

Unsuitable housing

Some housing may not be regarded by parents as being suitable for family life and this will put additional pressures on families.

The most significant way in which housing is likely to be regarded as unsuitable is through lack of space, or having no outside garden or play space, both problems associated with flats and maisonettes. For instance, on the South Bristol estates, where Barnardo's has been actively involved in community work for many years, there has historically been an imbalance of houses to flats for the composition of the population who have to live there. Many young families living on these estates are forced to bring up their children in cramped flats, without their own outside play space. This causes pressures for both children and parents and can increase levels of conflict within families. Overcrowding is associated with increased risks of both childhood accidents and ill health for parents and children.

In part, the lack of fit between what parents want and the housing they are offered is due to the changing aspirations and expectations of young families today, who are living on estates that were built in the 1950s and

1960s. But equally, this imbalance is the result of national policy. For instance, the 'right to buy' legislation has had a major impact on the provision of family housing since the 1980s. Almost all of the dwellings that have been sold to their tenants are the sought-after, three-bedroom family houses. By the late 1980s and early 1990s there was a marked imbalance in housing provision because the family homes that had been bought were often occupied by couples, or single people, whose children had left home. Many young families were, therefore, having to live in flats. It was not unusual for there to be a family with, say, three children living in a flat, in the same street as a single person living in a three-bedroom house bought under the 'right to buy' legislation.

Homelessness

Shelter estimates that over 100,000 children in England were homeless in 2002, with nearly 78,000 households living in temporary accommodation (Shelter, 2002a). Of particular concern were the number of families living in bed and breakfast accommodation, more than 12,000 in 2002, a 23 per cent increase on the previous year. This was obviously a concern shared by the government, which pledged to end all use of bed and breakfast accommodation for families by March 2004 (Shelter, 2002b).

It is important for assessments to acknowledge that homelessness is an experience that affects children and families who already have a number of serious problems. Vostanis and Cumella (1999) have pointed out that 'Homelessness has been seen almost entirely as a housing problem and there has been limited recognition of the overlap between the population of homeless families and the populations of children at risk, of children with mental health problems and of victims of domestic and neighbourhood violence' (p8).

The majority of families that are moved into temporary accommodation are moved to areas and neighbourhoods that are away from where they have previously lived. For instance, in London in the mid-1990s, as many as 60–70 per cent of homeless families with children were placed outside the local authority area responsible for providing them with accommodation (Royal College of Physicians, 1994). This tendency for accommodation to be provided away from the family's 'home' area has a number of important implications for children and parents. Amongst the most significant of these is the breakdown of contact with formal sources of help and support.

Moving area, as a result of homelessness, will also have important implications in terms of access to, and links with, health services. For families with young children it may lead to a disruption of contact with individual and trusted health visitors. Homelessness will therefore have strong connections with the extent of *social integration* and the access to *community resources*.

Experiencing a period of homelessness may also cause a breakdown of contact with informal sources of help and support. This will include contact with neighbours and other community members. It may also have implications for the lessening of ties with family members.

Also there is likely to be disruption to children's schooling. Because of the likelihood of moving area, the child in a family accepted as homeless may also have to move school. Research evidence indicates that such disruptions can have very significant and damaging effects on children's educational development. It may be important for workers involved in these situations to advocate strongly for the maintenance of continuity in schooling, especially if there is the eventual prospect of re-housing back in the original area. Practice evidence also shows that movement into and out of temporary accommodation may cause other problems. For example, it may mean that a child with a learning difficulty is not in one school long enough to complete the statementing process to assess their special educational needs.

Ensuring children continue to attend school makes particular demands on large families when they are made homeless. Power and her colleagues found that large families had difficulties in finding places for all their children in the same school. This led to additional demands not only in finding places, but also the extra time and cost in delivering and collecting children from their different schools (Power, Whitty and Yondall, 1999, pp131–2).

Some direct evidence of the impact of homelessness on children has come from recent work in Bristol (Shelter, 2002c). Children in homeless families missed their friends and worried about being bullied. Insecurity, fear, shame and anger were common emotions. Over half of the children in the study became noticeably more attention-seeking, and regressive behaviour, including bedwetting, was also in evidence. Aggression, even violence, was witnessed in some children, across all ages.

Homelessness can have other implications for children and families. It is likely, for instance, to put an extra strain on the family's financial resources.

There may be extra expenses involved, for example, in attempting to maintain social networks, using expensive public transport to visit family members and friends in previous areas of residence, or purchasing ready-made or take-away meals.

In addition, there is the evidence that homelessness and movement into temporary accommodation may undermine children's health and safety. Research in Reading, in the early 1990s, showed that 62 per cent of children in shared temporary accommodation had experienced acute upper respiratory infections in a four-week period. This compared with 12 per cent of 5–15-year-olds in the general population, over a two-week period (Davies, 1992).

There can also be serious risks posed to children's safety by dangerous adults, either living in the same shared accommodation, or in close proximity to it, often without anybody to warn the parents of the risks that their children might be facing.

Also, children in temporary accommodation are at greater risk of accidents in the home. In part, this may be the result of the increased levels of stress and insecurity that are likely to be experienced by parents and children in this situation. But equally, temporary accommodation can in itself be a more dangerous environment for children. For instance, shared kitchens, without eating space, mean that food often has to be transported from kitchens to bedrooms, perhaps necessitating carrying hot food up or down flights of stairs. Not surprisingly, research has shown that scalds and burns occur frequently in these circumstances (Families in Bayswater Bed and Breakfast, 1987). There is also the likelihood that the property will be in a less than satisfactory state of repair, with potentially dangerous windows, stairs and electrical equipment.

There is a real danger that any significant harm suffered by children in these circumstances might be misinterpreted by professionals as signs of either parental abuse or neglect, rather than the consequences of a dangerous environment which is not of the family's choosing.

Finally, it is important to realise that the impact of homelessness may still be significant long after the actual period of homelessness has come to an end. An experience of homelessness may have disrupted formal and informal networks of support and schooling in ways that continue to have implications long into the family's future.

Children with a disability or chronic illness

Specific assessment issues relating to the quality, suitability, location and appropriateness of housing are likely to arise when there is a disabled child, or a child with a chronic illness in the family.

It has been estimated that 1 in 10 children in the UK have a chronic illness that limits their day-to-day lives, and a further 3 per cent of children, aged between 5 and 15, will have a severe disability. Overall, there are estimated to be 150,000 families looking after a severely disabled child (Beresford and Oldman, 2000), and 360,000 children, with some form of disability, in the UK (Department of Health, 2000b). Although this latter figure is now somewhat out of date, being based on a survey carried out in 1989, it is still the one being relied upon by the government.

Once again, there are important interactions with the other categories on the bottom side of the triangle. For example, there is a close association between childhood disability, *family income* and *housing*: 'Disability is more likely to be found in low income groups and low income groups are more likely to live in rented properties. Generally families with disabled children are living in poorer quality housing (defined in terms of space standards, repair and environmental factors) than the rest of the population.' (Beresford and Oldman, 2000, p17). In an earlier study (Oldman and Beresford, 1998), the same researchers identified three key issues in relation to housing for disabled children:

- the low level of awareness, on the part of different professionals, about the importance of suitable housing for the health and well-being of disabled children and their families

- inadequate levels of funding for adapting unsuitable housing

- severe fragmentation of service provision for families with a disabled child.

Space is also likely to be an additional problem for families with a disabled child. Based on their research, Beresford and Oldman found that lack of space was a particular difficulty where the disabled child had behavioural and/or sleep problems, because other family members needed opportunities for 'physical and psychological space', away from the disabled child (Beresford and Oldman, 2000, p36).

Housing and education

We have already discussed the impact that homelessness can have on the education of children. There are, however, wider links between housing provision and education that may need to be considered in assessments of children in need.

The process of residualisation, referred to at the beginning of the chapter, generates areas with concentrations of social difficulties that affect a wide range of local services and environmental conditions, including the intake of pupils to local schools. A study in the North East of England adopted a case study approach, to one local primary school that served an area of social housing, in order to examine how the school was being affected by gradual changes in housing allocations (Clark, Dyson and Millward, 1999). The researchers found that an increasing proportion of the young children entering the school were less ready for formal education and that more of them subsequently had problems with literacy and displayed disruptive behaviour. It was also apparent that it was becoming increasingly difficult for the school to enlist the support and co-operation of parents in their children's education.

This study showed that it took relatively small increases in the numbers of families with these extra difficulties to de-stabilise the school's functioning. The initial response of the school and other agencies in the area was to single out the individual children with extra needs as 'the problem'. Their families tended either to already be alienated from potential resources in the community, or were being dealt with, on an individual, case-by-case basis, by the different agencies. This approach failed to recognise the part played by housing allocations in creating the difficulties that were arising. The researchers identified a clear need for the school to work more collaboratively with the wider community and for the social landlord responsible for housing allocations on the estate to work more closely with the local school and other agencies.

Issues for assessment

Housing issues are typically given very limited attention in assessments of children in need. In part this is because of the general reluctance of workers and their managers and employing agencies to consider the structural determinants of parenting capacity and children's development. In addition, workers have been given few guidelines or models for understanding the impact of housing on families. The level of analysis is therefore very limited and either concentrates on overcrowding issues or sees housing conditions more as a reflection of parenting capacity, rather than the other way around. Also workers may see themselves as relatively powerless in influencing housing resources and will therefore concentrate on the interpersonal aspects of family life.

However, if workers develop real partnerships with parents and understand their interpretation of their difficulties, housing is likely to play a much more significant role in assessments. Not only will the inadequacy of housing provision frequently present direct difficulties in the day-to-day tasks of bringing up children, its impact on children can also be indirect but nevertheless very powerful. If parents are under pressure and experience stress in their accommodation and its location then this pressure will often contribute to a failure to cope with the demands of childcare and significant levels of depression.

Assessment based on an ecological approach should draw attention to housing at three different levels. First, it should look at the adequacy of the housing in terms of the family's needs. This is a much wider question than merely the level of overcrowding. It involves issues of access to play, safety issues and a sense of security. Second, it should look at how housing and its location structures human relationships – how it supports or is detrimental to networks. And third, it should examine how the family themselves perceive their accommodation.

Central to an ecological perspective will also be the links between housing and the other assessment categories on the bottom side of the triangle. For instance housing will be directly influenced by the family's *income* and *employment* situation. Housing provision and the cost of housing will also, in turn, affect the amount of money that families have at their disposal. Equally, there will be links with *community resources*. The same type of accommodation can be viewed very differently by families if it is in an area where there are developed and relevant *community resources*, rather than in an area where there are very limited or poor quality resources.

In a more general way, housing provision will be a key determinant of *social integration*. It will impact on networks of support and the child's friendship and peer relations. Equally it will impact on contact with *wider family* members and the support that they in turn can give. If, for instance, there are mixed types of tenancy and sizes of property in an area, this will play a part in facilitating relationships across the generations.

References

Beresford, B and Oldman, C (2000) *Making Homes Fit for Children*. York: Joseph Rowntree Foundation

Blackburn, C (1991) *Poverty and Health: Working with families*. Buckingham: Open University Press

Brown, GW and Harris, T (1978) *The Social Origins of Depression*. London: Tavistock

Burrows R (1999) Residential mobility and residualisation in social housing in England. *Journal of Social Policy*, **28**(1), 27–52

Clark, J, Dyson, A, Millward, A (1999) *Housing and Schooling: A case-study in joined up problems*. York: York Publishing Services

Davie, CE, Hutt, SJ, Vincent, E, Mason, M (1984) *The Young Child at Home*. Windsor: NFER – Nelson

Davies, E (1992) *The Health of Homeless and Hidden Homeless Families in Reading*, Reading Borough Council and West Berks Health Authority, quoted in K Hutchinson (1999) Health problems of homeless children, pp28–42 in Vostanis and Cumella, as below

Department of Health (2000a) *Children Act Report 1995–1999*. London: The Stationery Office

Department of Health (2000b) *Framework for the Assessment of Children in Need and their Families: The family pack of questionnaires and scales*. London: The Stationery Office

Families in Bayswater Bed and Breakfast (1987) *Speaking for Ourselves*. London: The Bayswater Hotel Homeless Project quoted in K Hutchinson (1999), Health problems of homeless children, pp28–42 in Vostanis and Cumella, as below

Forrest, R and Murie, A (1995) Accumulating evidence: housing and family wealth in Britain. In R Forrest and A Murie (eds) *Housing and Family Wealth: Comparative international perspectives*, pp58–85. London: Routledge

Hills, J (2001) 'Inclusion or exclusion? The role of housing subsidies and benefits. *Urban Studies*, **38**(11), 1887–902

Kemp, R and Fordham, G (1997) *Going the Extra Mile. Implementing 'housing plus' on five London housing association estates*. York: Joseph Rowntree Foundation

Lakey, J (1997) Neighbourhoods and housing. In T Modood and R Berthoud, pp184–223, as below

Lee, P and Murie, A (1997) *Poverty, Housing Tenure and Social Exclusion*. Bristol: The Policy Press

Malpass, P and Murie, A (1999) *Housing Policy and Practice* (5th edn) Basingstoke: Macmillan

Malpass, P (1990) *Reshaping Housing Policy: Subsidies, Rent and Residualisation*. London: Routledge

Modood, T and Berthoud, R (1997) *Ethnic Minorities in Britain. Diversity and disadvantage*. London: Policy Studies Institute

Morris, J and Winn, M (1990) *Housing and Social Inequality*. London: Hilary Shipman

Oldman, C and Beresford, B (1998) *Homes Unfit for Children. Housing, disabled children and their families*. Bristol: The Policy Press

Packman, J with Randall, J and Jacques, N (1986) *Who Needs Care? Social work decisions about children*. Oxford: Blackwell

Platt, S (1989) Damp housing, mould growth and symptomatic health state. *British medical Journal*, **298**, 1673–8. Quoted in Blackburn, as above

Power, S, Whitty, G, Yondell, D (1999) Doubly disadvantaged: education and the homeless child, pp130–141 in Vostanis and Cumella, as below

Royal College of Physicians (1994) *Homelessness and Ill Health*. London: Royal College of Physicians. Quoted in J Barnes (1999) in Vostanis and Cumella, as below

Royal Society for the Prevention of Accidents (1998) Press release, 13 August

Shelter (2002a) *No Room to Play*, http://www.shelter.org.uk/campaign/features/noroomtoplay/index.asp

Shelter (2002b) Shelter Press Release, http://www.shelter.org.uk/about/press/viewpressrelease.asp

Shelter (2002c) *Where's Home? Children and homelessness in Bristol*. London: Shelter

Somerville, P and Steele, A (eds) (2002) *'Race', Housing and Social Exclusion*. London: Jessica Kingsley

Speak, S (1995) *The Difficulties of Setting up Home for Young Single Mothers*. York: Joseph Rowntree Foundation

Vostanis, P and Cumella, S (1999) *Homeless Children: Problems and needs*. London: Jessica Kingsley

Wilkinson, D (1999) *Poor Housing and Ill Health: A summary of research evidence*. Edinburgh: Scottish Office Central Research University

Wider family 7

The network of relationships that exist between parents and children, on the one hand, and members of their wider family, on the other, are likely to exert a profound influence on children's development and the capacity of parents to successfully raise their children. Most of the literature on this subject incorporates considerations of the influence of wider family relationships on parents and children within overall social support networks, including relationships with friends, neighbours, colleagues and professionals. For this reason, it is important to read this chapter in conjunction with the chapter on *social integration*, which considers the influence of social support from non-relatives on parents and children. In both of these chapters we use the available evidence to reveal how different types of social support tend to be provided by different types of network members, with some significant differences between kin and non-kin (Gill et al, 2000; Wellman and Wortley, 1990; Gibbons, 1990; Fischer, 1982).

As throughout the rest of this volume, we highlight the way that wider family relationships interact with other factors, such as ethnic background, *family history and functioning*, family structure, and geographical proximity (which is often linked to issues of *housing* and *employment*). We also caution against simplistic assumptions about the positive influence of wider family networks. Perhaps even more than relationships with non-relatives, those with wider family members have the potential to be either supportive or undermining, often combining aspects of both.

The chapter begins with a detailed consideration of the wider family networks of parents and then children. It also examines some of the ways in which a growing acknowledgement of the importance of wider family relationships, for both parents and children, is now influencing social work practice. In particular we focus on the growing acceptance of the place of family group conferences in decision-making and planning for children and families, the role of kinship care (ie out-of-home placements with relatives), and the maintenance of wider family relationships for children who cannot live with their own parents. The chapter concludes with a section identifying the main issues for assessments in relation to wider family members.

The wider family networks of parents

There is a substantial body of research evidence, from around the world, that clearly demonstrates the importance of different kinds of relationships for personal well-being (eg, Dunst, Leet and Trivette, 1988; Hashima and Amato, 1994). Relationships that are perceived to be either potential, or actual, sources of information and advice, practical help, or emotional support, have consistently been found to be associated with a range of positive influences on parents and children. Conversely, a lack of social support, or social isolation, is consistently linked with poorer personal health and child neglect (Blaxter, 1990; Coohey, 1996; Thompson, 1995). Relationships between adult partners within families tend to exert the strongest influences, followed by those with close relatives beyond the household, and then friends, neighbours and lay or professional helpers, usually in that order (Bronfenbrenner, 1986; Gibbons, 1990).

Amongst wider family relationships, it is usually those between parents and their own parents, particularly their mothers, which are the most important. For example, in a study conducted by one of the authors and his colleagues with parents (mainly mothers) of young children in a disadvantaged area of Bristol, they identified their own parents as their most significant sources of virtually every dimension of social support (Gill, Tanner and Bland, 2000). The different types of support most commonly provided by (or potentially available from) their own mothers included advice about children's behaviour, personal relationships and financial problems, and practical help with material goods and childcare. The only aspects of social support in which this relationship was not preeminent were advice on children's behaviour, where health visitors were equally consulted, and emotional support in relation to 'private' matters, when close friends were slightly more likely to be involved. The mothers' adult siblings and other relatives were also perceived to be important sources of all types of social support by the majority of respondents. For the majority of mothers in this study, a picture of regular contact with local kin emerged, despite high levels of family breakdown, with 40 per cent of the respondents (and half of their parents' generation) having experienced separation or divorce. In this locality, the problems came for the minority of parents who did not have access to (supportive) local kin, because *community resources* for families with children were poorly developed. There were also links to *social integration* because the families who had limited parental support were often also those who were less established in the neighbourhood, having moved home recently.

The importance of wider family support for parenting is particularly evident in relation to the increasing emphasis on women taking up paid *employment* outside the household. In the current context of limited affordable childcare, particularly in more disadvantaged and rural areas, there is an inevitable pressure on wider family members, especially grandparents, to assume caring responsibilities for children. It has been estimated, by Age Concern, that nearly half of all childcare in the UK is now provided by grandparents (*Guardian*, 2000). Also, an ICM Poll found that over one third of grandparents spend more than 21 hours a week caring for their grandchildren, and over a quarter spend more than 26 hours a week doing so (*Guardian*, 2000b). However, findings from the annual British Social Attitudes Survey (National Centre for Social Research, 1999) reveal that, whilst many grandparents are indeed involved in providing some childcare for working parents, there are limits to what they are willing and able to provide. The survey reveals that the highest level of grandparental care was actually provided for the 40 per cent of mothers who worked part time. Nearly a third of grandparents with a grandchild under 13 provided day-time childcare at least once a week to help a mother working part time. This compares to only a fifth who provided such help to mothers working full time, and less than a sixth for mothers who were not working outside the home. However, as we pointed out in the introduction to this chapter, it is also important to recognise that members of the wider family may represent a drain on parental resources, rather than a support to them. For instance, a grandparent who is ill, or going through relationship difficulties, or starting another family, may represent a significant source of pressure on the parent.

Research from the USA reveals significant racial and ethnic differences in views about the appropriateness of using kin-based care to support parents going out to work. A study of 31 racially diverse employed mothers found that variations in the use of and preference for relative care was associated with a range of factors. These included the belief that parents should be caring for their own children, the proximity of relatives able and willing to undertake childcare, family income, maternal level of education, single-parent status and the ages and number of the children involved. The study found that rates of relative care of children, to support parents in work, were higher among black and Hispanic families than among white families, due to a combination of cultural and structural factors. Black and Hispanic families showed both a greater cultural acceptance of relatives providing childcare, and a wider pool of available relatives, whose more limited employment opportunities placed parents under an obligation to utilise them for paid childcare, even if their own individual preferences and financial means might otherwise have led them to choose professional carers (Uttal, 1999).

In addition to these variations, research also shows that, for most parents, care by relatives is seen either as a back-up to more formal full-time arrangements with commercial daycarers, or as a time-limited arrangement to support less frequent work commitments. As we would expect, within the ecological model, the particular arrangements that emerge in individual circumstances will be the outcome of a wide range of interacting factors, such as *family history* and *wider family* networks, geographical proximity, the nature of the *employment*, the level of family *income*, the availability of *community resources* (in the form of childcare facilities and transport) and the family's level of *social integration* in their local neighbourhood. It will also be dependent on the individual characteristics of both the parents and the children concerned. For example, it is well known that the employment opportunities for parents with a child who has a significant disability are more restricted, partly as a result of the greater difficulties in finding suitable daycare for children with disabilities (Joseph Rowntree Foundation, 1999).

The wider family networks of children

Like adult networks, those of children are also influenced by a range of interacting factors, such as their age, gender, culture, family structure, and social class. The interaction of a range of ecological factors with children's wider family relationships is well illustrated by a comparative study of the social networks of children growing up either in the suburbs of a large Swedish city, or in a village in Papua New Guinea (Tietjen, 1989). On average, the Swedish children named fewer than two adult relatives and fewer than one child relative, outside their household, in their social network, compared to an average of more than ten adult and more than ten child relatives named by the Papuan children. The different size of these children's wider family networks reflects major differences based not just on physical proximity but also on different cultural conceptions about family membership and the importance of wider family relationships.

For child welfare staff undertaking assessments, it is important to realise that children's relationships with wider family members change over time. This is clearly demonstrated in a range of studies, such as a longitudinal study of 75 North American children (mainly living in two-parent families of European descent) with data collected when the children were aged 3, 6 and 9 years. The study revealed that the proportion of relatives to non-relatives in the children's networks declined with the child's increasing age, as did the amount of contact the children had with members of their wider family. Girls, however, maintained more contact with relatives than boys, at all three ages (Feiring and Lewis, 1989). Another study, also conducted in the USA, examined the networks of older children (Furman, 1989). Here, children's increasing age was found to be associated with declining levels of perceived support from wider family members (grandparents), as well as parents and siblings. In other words, these changes are a normal consequence of development across childhood, and are not restricted to relationships with wider family members but apply to all kin relationships. Interestingly, the advent of higher education, usually accompanied by a move out of the family household (at least during term-time) was accompanied by the perception that parental and sibling relationships were more supportive again, but not those with grandparents. Data from the US Longitudinal Study of Generations (Silverstein and Long, 1998) also reveals the way that grandparent–grandchild relationships change over the lifecourse, tending to be at their strongest when both are younger, declining in terms of proximity and contact, over time. This study also suggests that more recent cohorts of the population show steeper declines than previous generations, suggesting that factors such as rising levels of health, income, mobility and family breakdown are influencing the lifecourse development of children's wider family relationships. Whilst all of this information is drawn from US studies, there is no reason to believe that the same general trends would not be found in the UK, if similar research were undertaken here.

In the UK context, we know that grandparents, along with other relatives, can play an especially important role in the lives of children experiencing particular difficulties within their families. For example, only a small minority of children whose parents have separated think that they were given a proper explanation by their parents about the break-up. Often it is their grandparents who are their main confidants at this time. A close relationship with the child's maternal grandparents appears to offer particular protection against the potentially harmful effects on the development of such children experiencing family disruptions, being associated with less anxiety and aggression, fewer school and relationship problems, and better long-term adjustment (Dunn and Deater-Deckard, 2001). This ties in with other studies examining the resilience of some children, who are able to cope successfully with difficult events or circumstances in their lives because of supportive relationships with their grandparents (Gilligan, 2001). In terms of assessment, it is also important to be alive to the possibility that, in spite of family change and disruption, children will often maintain contact with an absent parent's relatives. For instance, Gill and his colleagues found that a significant number of the children in the single-mother households that they studied continued to have regular contact with their paternal grandparents (Gill, Tanner and Bland, 2000). This underlines the importance of looking beyond the relatives of current household members when wider family networks are being considered.

In fact, one of the strongest and most consistent findings in this area of research, for children living in difficult family circumstances, is the protective influence of a positive and enduring relationship with a caring adult outside their household (Bronfenbrenner, 1986; Gibbons, 1990; Werner and Smith, 1992; Gilligan, 1999). For all children, belonging to a network of family relationships, that reaches beyond their immediate household, helps to promote their sense of identity and belonging, as well as being linked to the development of self-esteem and self-efficacy (Rutter, 1990). These are also important components of resilience for children living in adverse circumstances. A longitudinal study conducted by researchers at the University of Michigan provides evidence of the way in which children's developing self-esteem is linked to their family's integration into their wider family networks (Yabiku, Axinn and Thornton, 1999). For children, feeling that they are part of a caring group of (related) people, who are interested in their long-term well-being, and who participate in intergenerational social and material exchanges that regularly demonstrate this interest, is a crucial element in the development of their self-image. Important variables for child (and eventual adult) outcomes will, of course, concern not just the strength of these relationships, but the values, beliefs and behaviour of the individuals who comprise the wider family network.

There is therefore ample evidence of both the positive and negative influences that wider family networks have upon children's development, including many of the sorts of family situations which social workers are likely to be dealing with that involve intergenerational aspects of the development of such behaviours as child abuse and criminality (Oliver, 1993; Monk, 1996; Rutter, Giller and Hagell, 1998). The important points for practice are to recognise the positive potential of supportive wider family relationships for all children, whilst at the same time making a detailed assessment of both the positive and negative influences of particular relationships on individual children's development.

Three-generation households

So far, our consideration of wider family relationships has focused exclusively on the influence of relatives outside the household. However, there are also a small number of households that include other adult relatives, as well as children and their parents. Whilst their absolute numbers are small, they are worthy of special attention because of what they can reveal about the variable impact, on different household members, of what, at first sight, might appear to be similar circumstances. In other words, they can remind us of the need to look at families not so much as homogeneous units, but rather as complex systems of interacting individuals, who are likely to have very different needs, roles and aspirations.

First of all, it is interesting to note that three-generation households can have beneficial effects for children's development, particularly in contexts where such arrangements represent either a cultural norm, or where they can provide added protection against the potentially harmful influences of impoverished environments (Al Awad and Sonuga-Barke, 1992; Chase-Lansdale, Brooks-Gunn and Zamsky, 1994). The direct benefits for children include some of those that we have already seen they can derive from close, supportive relationships with wider family members, outside their household, particularly grandparents. Children can also benefit indirectly from the support that parents may receive with parenting tasks from wider family members living in the household, such as advice and information, practical help with childcare, and emotional support. However, in situations where the presence of grandparents in the household is perceived by parents to be a source of stress and conflict, rather than help and support, the outcomes for both parents and children are likely to be less favourable (Chase-Lansdale, Brooks-Gunn and Zamsky 1994; Unger and Cooley, 1992).

In a UK study, comparing two- and three-generation Muslim and Hindu families, the mental health of mothers and grandmothers, and the development of children aged 5–11 years, were examined. In both the Muslim and Hindu three-generation households, the children and their grandmothers were found to be doing better than their counterparts in nuclear families but, unfortunately, the reverse was true for the mothers (Sonuga-Barke and Mistry, 2000). The researchers concluded that this was because the grandmothers living in three-generation households were better able to fulfil their traditional role, which both enhanced their own self-worth and enabled their presence in the household to produce beneficial effects on their grandchildren's development. However, the role demands, intergenerational tensions and potential disagreements over child-rearing, experienced by the mothers in these three-generation households, resulted in higher levels of maternal depression and anxiety than was found among mothers in two-generation households. Interestingly, the personal costs borne by three-generation household mothers were not having the sort of detrimental effects on children's development that would be found in nuclear family arrangements, perhaps because of the protective influence of the presence of a grandmother in the household on the children.

If nothing else, this sort of evidence should alert us to the dangers inherent in making over-simplistic assumptions about the supportive potential of wider family relationships, especially when ill-informed generalisations about culture and ethnic background are also present. For example, there is a considerable body of evidence that challenges commonly held assumptions about the support resources available to minority ethnic families living in the UK. What this evidence reveals is that factors such as geographical isolation, restricted income, and antipathy about asking for help from other hard-pressed family members, often leaves minority ethnic families with significant deficits in their wider family support resources. This is especially true when they have additional needs themselves, such as caring for a severely disabled child (Chamba et al, 1999). Once again, the clear messages here are about avoiding assumptions and ensuring that detailed and holistic assessments, based on an understanding of the complex interaction of a range of ecological factors, are undertaken.

Family group decision-making and planning

'... given the resources, the information and the power, a family group will make safe and appropriate decisions for children.' (quoted in Ryburn and Atherton, 1996, p17)

This is an extract from the briefing paper produced by the New Zealand government, to accompany the introduction of the Children, Young Persons and their Families Act 1989, which placed what they called family group conferences at the heart of decision-making for both child welfare and youth justice cases. Between the passing of the Act and 1998, more than 22,000 such conferences had been held in New Zealand (Marsh and Crow, 1998), and the model has been introduced in many other developed countries in the English-speaking world, including the USA, Canada, Australia and the UK (Maluccio, Ainsworth and Thoburn, 2000). The model was originally developed in New Zealand, in response to growing concerns about over-intrusive state interventions into families that tended to exclude family members from an active role in decision-making. This resulted in large numbers of children being placed in institutional care or with unrelated carers. Particular criticism of these policies and outcomes were voiced by the Maori community, which raised its concerns about the over-representation of Maori children in state care and the way that the existing processes failed to take account of the central role of the family in making decisions about children. A number of authors have drawn attention to similar criticisms and processes of reform in the other countries that have since adopted some form of family group decision-making into their own child welfare and youth justice systems (Marsh and Crow, 1998; Jackson and Nixon, 1999).

In England and Wales, the introduction of the Children Act 1989 was accompanied by a number of pilot projects, supported by the Family Rights Group, designed to test out the family group conference approach in the UK context. However, unlike in New Zealand, the use of family group conferences is not a legislative requirement, although its principles do not conflict in any significant way with the Children Act. Whilst these pilot projects, and various other initiatives that have followed them, vary in small ways from one another, the basic principles of the model are the same in nearly all projects. The process initially involves referral of cases to an independent co-ordinator who, in consultation with all relevant persons, identifies who is to be invited (including the child, immediate and wider family members, and other non-relatives significant to the family) and the time and venue for the meeting. The co-ordinator also undertakes any preparation of family members and professionals attending the meeting that may be necessary. The meeting itself, which is chaired by the co-ordinator, falls into three distinct phases, the first of which involves the professionals at the meeting sharing information with the family group about their concerns for the child and the type and level of resources available. The family group members can ask questions before the professionals withdraw. During the second phase of the meeting the family group is left in private (usually with the co-ordinator and other key professionals available for consultation, if desired) to draw up a plan designed to ensure the child's (or the community's) future safety and well-being. The professionals only rejoin the meeting, for the final phase of its deliberations, when the family group are ready. Normally, the only grounds for refusing a plan in child welfare cases are either if it would place the child at continuing risk of significant harm, or if the resources required are not available. In youth justice cases, a plan could also be refused if it failed to address the risk of future offending, or the needs of the victim(s) (Jackson and Nixon, 1999).

Evaluations of this approach, in all the countries in which it is either fully operational or being piloted, have been very positive in terms of participant satisfaction ratings. In England and Wales, the national summary of the pilot project evaluations (Crow and Marsh, 1997) found that levels of satisfaction among family participants were between 75 and 80 per cent. This is very similar to the satisfaction levels found in Victoria, Australia (Swain and Ban, 1997), although the level of satisfaction does tend to decline with the passage of time. For example, there was a fall from 90 per cent, immediately after the conferences held in one of the pilot areas (Hampshire), to 56 per cent three months afterwards (Jackson and Nixon, 1999). However, this is still a substantially higher level of satisfaction than is found in traditional decision-making processes involving child protection conferences and criminal courts (eg, see Cleaver and Freeman, 1995). Two-thirds of the social workers involved in the national evaluations in England and Wales also thought that the children were better protected by the plans made at family group conferences than they would otherwise have been (Crow and Marsh, 1997). There is also clear evidence, from New Zealand and elsewhere, of the influence of this approach in significantly reducing the number of children and young people who enter state care and custody (Ryburn, 1993; Maxwell and Morris, 1993), and facilitating the care of an increased proportion of children by relatives, when they cannot remain with their own parents (Crow and Marsh, 1997).

However, despite such evidence of the positive potential of involving wider family members in decision-making and planning for children, the family group approach is certainly no panacea. It requires the availability of skilled co-ordinators and the provision of sufficient resources that are also flexible enough to support even the most unconventional plans. There have also been concerns expressed, by some professionals, about the potential of this approach to fail to effectively challenge the power differentials (based on patriarchy) within families, particularly where sexual abuse by male family members of female and child members of the family network is a factor. However, evidence from one of the English pilot projects indicates that women are usually very satisfied with the plans agreed (Lupton and Stevens, 1997). There is also evidence of women using family group conferences to establish coalitions with other members of the family network to improve children's safety (Ryburn and Atherton, 1996), a process that has been referred to as 'ally location' (Hamill, 1996).

Kinship care and family contact for looked-after children

As already indicated, the development of the family group conference model, combined with research evidence and legislative changes, together have produced an increasing interest in kinship care (ie out-of-home placements with relatives) and an awareness of the importance of maintaining wider family relationships for children who are looked after by local authorities.

In the UK, whilst only a small proportion of children officially 'looked after' by local authorities are placed with wider family members (about 7.5 per cent in 1997), a much higher proportion of children, who never enter the formal care system, are actually living with relatives other than their parents (Maluccio, Ainsworth and Thoburn, 2000). A number of researchers in the UK have drawn attention to the relatively small proportion of local authority placements of children with relatives. This is surprising, given the strong and consistent evidence of the better outcomes that such placements appear to provide for the children who experience them, compared to otherwise similar children placed with unrelated foster carers or living in residential homes (Rowe et al, 1984; Berridge and Cleaver, 1987; Berridge, 1997). For example, in Berridge and Cleaver's study of children in planned long-term placements, the breakdown rate in kinship–care placements was only 8 per cent, compared to 38 per cent among the general sample. This is especially significant when it is realised that the children placed with relatives tend to be older at the time of placement and also to bring with them more complex problems.

The majority of kinship placements in the Rowe study were with grandparents (42 per cent), with a smaller proportion being with an aunt (22 per cent) or a sister (8 per cent). This meant that, on average, the carers tended to be older than non-relative foster carers. Other research with grandparent carers reveals their worries about their age, which they fear might prevent them from being there to help their grandchildren in the future (Family Rights Group, 2001). Other problems facing relatives looking after children, identified in a study of 50 kinship placements in Wandsworth (Broad, Hayes and Rushforth, 2001), included financial problems – many are pensioners with no capacity to increase their income and able to get very little help, in most cases, from their local authorities – overcrowding, ill health, and loss of freedom and independence. However, the carers were almost unanimous in their love and commitment towards the children (and their parents), stressing the importance of providing a home that allowed children to maintain their place in the family. In all but one case, the carers also exactly matched the child's ethnic origins. These findings were also reflected in interviews with 22 of the young people involved in the study. Many of them expressed a sense of 'emotional permanence' within their kinship placements, although some were also experiencing the financial and autonomy problems highlighted by their carers.

One aspect of kinship care that has caused some concern, however, involves the lower proportion of such placements that eventually result in the child's reunification with their parents. For example, Rowe found that only a third of relative placements ended in this outcome, compared to over half of those leaving unrelated foster carers (Rowe, Hundleby and Garrett, 1989). Similar findings have emerged from comparative studies in the United States (see Maluccio, Ainsworth and Thoburn, 2000 for a summary). However, these different outcomes can largely be explained by differences in the populations of children using these placements and in the aims of the placements themselves. The aim of the majority of kinship placements in the Rowe study, for example, was long-term care and upbringing, rather than temporary care with a view to eventual return home, and we have already noted the more difficult family problems that tend to characterise the children who go to live with relatives.

For those children who do spend time living away from their parents, especially those who are in non-relative placements, the research evidence is very clear that the maintenance of family relationships (particularly with parents and siblings) is associated with the chances of children returning home (Fratter *et al*, 1991; Millham *et al*, 1986). In addition, contrary to popular assumptions, there is no evidence that parental contact, where it is not detrimental to the welfare of the child, destabilises placements (Berridge, 1997). In recognition of this sort of research evidence, the Children Act 1989 introduced a duty on local authorities to promote contact with family members for 'looked-after' children, wherever this would not threaten the welfare of the child. However, practice evidence suggests that this duty has largely failed to ensure that the needs of children to maintain contact with wider family members (beyond parents and siblings) is given the priority it deserves.

There are local examples of which we are aware in which financial constraints on local authority budgets have led them to interpret the duty to promote contact in a very narrow way that excludes, for example, assistance with transport costs. Clearly, some of the barriers to maintaining contact identified in the well-known Dartington study in the mid-1980s (Millham et al, 1986), are sadly still in evidence today.

Issues for assessment

The inclusion of the wider family dimension within the Assessment Framework is a reminder to anyone working with children in need and their families of the central importance of relatives to both parents and children. Whilst full consideration of wider family networks has been an integral part of foster carer and adoptive parent assessments for many years, unfortunately the same could not always be said for much of mainstream childcare practice, before the introduction of the new Assessment Framework.

For parents, assessments of children in need should now always include a consideration of the relatives who make up their wider families and those members of the network with whom parents are in regular contact. The assessment will not only need to identify who is in the wider family network, but also to understand the nature and quality of those relationships. For example, are particular relationships supportive of parenting tasks, or do they tend to be characterised more by their capacity to undermine parenting, because of the level of conflict or criticism that they involve? If they are potentially supportive, how accessible and reliable are they and what particular kinds of social support can they offer? For example, practical help with childcare, either on a regular basis, or at times of crisis, may be a crucial component of successful parenting, for either working parents or those who are living in particularly stressful environments. Alternatively, as we consider in Chapter 4 on income, relatives may play a vital role in providing additional financial resources for hard-pressed families. Relatives are also likely to play an important role in providing advice and information on parenting issues, as well as supporting parents emotionally.

If parents are geographically or emotionally isolated from sources of support from within their wider family, as is the case, for example, for many families of minority ethnic background living in the UK, assessments will need to be accompanied by plans that can enhance the resilience of the family. These plans might involve, for example, therapeutic work on relationships designed to reduce the conflict between parents and significant relatives. Alternatively, the support that could be offered by a relative might need to be unlocked by the provision of services to the relative, rather than to the parent. If these sorts of options are not feasible, workers and families may need to turn their attentions towards enhancing the support that parents can access or develop from non-relatives (see Chapter 2 on social integration).

Assessments of wider family networks also need to include children's own relationships with relatives outside their household. The primary focus of much childcare work is likely to involve how to deal with the presence of one or more dangerous adults within the family networks of children at risk of significant harm. In these cases, assessments may lead to interventions designed to enhance the capacity of non-abusing adult members of the family network to protect the child in the future (see, for example, Smith, 1994). Beyond such immediate protection issues, workers will need to communicate directly with children in order to identify any supportive relationships with wider family members. Children will need to be helped to identify and describe relationships, enabling them to explore their qualities and the influence that they have on their daily life, including their behaviour, attitudes, identity and self-esteem. In particular, for children in need living in adverse family circumstances, assessments should be trying to identify any 'special' relationships that the child has with particular relatives outside their immediate family. These might be relationships on which the child is relying for their day-to-day survival and developmental progress (eg, support for their education, or important activities), or that are important for their sense of belonging and identity. Or they might be relationships that they feel they can fall back on, or escape to, at particularly difficult times in their home life. The task for the worker, having identified any such relationships, is to ensure that they are properly recognised in decisions affecting the child and that they are supported and nurtured, as appropriate, in order to enhance the child's resilience.

In fact, the importance of wider family relationships needs to be a central theme in *any* significant decisions made in connection with children in need. Workers and their managers need to ask themselves if everything possible is being done to ensure that all the significant members of a child's wider family are appropriately involved in assessment and planning processes. If a family group conference model is not part of local policy, can any of the principles of inclusion of wider family members, that underpin this approach, be adopted in individual cases, or in the way that the team works? Have the options for placement with relatives been fully considered if the child cannot remain at home? If the child is already in a kinship placement, is the local authority responsible doing everything that is required to support the placement, especially in relation to financial support? And finally, for looked-after children, especially those who are living with unrelated carers, have appropriate plans been made to promote contact with significant members of their wider family network, again including provision for financial support, where this would be helpful? These are the types of issues that need to be on the agenda of all assessments of children in need if the aspirations of the Assessment Framework, to incorporate wider family issues into an overall ecological model, are to be realised.

References

Al Awad, A and Sonuga-Barke, E (1992) Childhood problems in a Sudanese city: a comparison of extended and nuclear families. *Child Development,* **63**, 907–14

Berridge, D (1997) *Foster Care: A research review.* London: The Stationery Office

Berridge, D and Cleaver, H (1987) *Foster Home Breakdown.* Oxford: Blackwell

Blaxter, M (1990) *Health and Lifestyles.* London: Routledge

Broad, B, Hayes, R, Rushforth, C (2001) *Kith and Kin: Kinship care for vulnerable young people.* London: National Children's Bureau

Bronfenbrenner, U (1986) Ecology of the family as a context for human development: research perspectives. *Developmental Psychology,* **22**(6), 723–42

Chamba, R, Ahmad, W, Hirst, M, Lawton, D, Beresford, B (1999) *On the Edge: Minority ethnic families caring for a severely disabled child.* London: The Policy Press

Chase-Lansdale, PL, Brooks-Gunn, J, Zamsky, ES (1994) Young African-American multigenerational families in poverty: quality of mothering and grandmothering. *Child Development,* **65**, 373–93

Cleaver, H and Freeman, P (1995) *Parental Perspectives in Cases of Suspected Child Abuse.* London: HMSO

Coohey, C (1996) Child maltreatment: testing the social isolation hypothesis. *Child Abuse and Neglect,* **20**(3), 241–54

Crow, G and Marsh, P (1997) *Family Group Conferences, Partnership and Child Welfare: A research report on four pilot projects in England and Wales.* Sheffield: University of Sheffield Partnership Research Programme

Dunn, J and Deater-Deckard, K (2001) *Children's Views of their Changing Families.* York: York Publishing Services

Dunst, CJ, Leet, HE, Trivette, CM (1988) Family resources, personal wellbeing and early intervention. *Journal of Special Education*, **22**, 108–16

Family Rights Group (2001) *Second Time Around*. London: Family Rights Group

Feiring, C and Lewis, M (1989) The social networks of girls and boys from early through middle childhood. In D Belle (ed) *Children's Social Networks and Social Supports*, pp119–50. New York: Wiley

Fischer, C (1982) *To Dwell Among Friends: Personal networks in town and city*. Chicago: Chicago University Press

Fratter, J, Rowe, J, Sapsford, P, Thoburn J (1991) *Permanent Family Placement: A decade of experience*. London: BAAF

Furman, W (1989) The development of children's social networks. In D Belle (ed) *Children's Social Networks and Social Supports*, pp151–72. New York: Wiley

Gibbons, J (1990) *Family Support and Prevention: Studies in local areas*. London: HMSO

Gill, O, Tanner, C, Bland, L (2000) *Family Support: Strengths and pressures in a 'high risk' neighbourhood*. Barkingside: Barnardo's

Gilligan, R (1999) Children's own social networks and network members: key resources in helping children at risk. In M Hill (ed) *Effective Ways of Helping Children*. London: Jessica Kingsley

Gilligan, R (2001) Promoting positive outcomes for children in need: the asessment of protective factors. In J Horwath (ed) *The Child's World: Assessing children in need*. London: Jessica Kingsley

Guardian (2000) Here We Go Again, December 14

Hamill, H (1996) *Family Group Conferences in Child Care Practice*. Norwich: University of East Anglia

Hashima, PY, and Amato, PR (1994) Poverty, social support and parental behaviour, *Child Development*, **65**, 394–403

Jackson, S and Nixon, P (1999) Family group conferences: a challenge to the old order? In L Dominelli (ed) *Community Approaches to Child Welfare: International perspectives*. Aldershot: Ashgate Publishing, pp117–146

Joseph Rowntree Foundation (1999) *Supporting Disabled Children and their Families*. York: Joseph Rowntree Foundation

Lupton, C and Stevens, M (1997) *Family Outcomes: Following through on family social conferences*, Report No.34. Social Services Research and Information Unit, University of Portsmouth

Maluccio, AN, Ainsworth, F, Thoburn, J (2000) *Child Welfare Outcome Research in the United States, the United Kingdom and Australia*. Washington, DC: Child Welfare League of America

Marsh, P and Crow, G (1998) *Family Group Conferences in Child Welfare*. Oxford: Blackwell

Maxwell, GM and Morris, A (1993) *Families, Victims and Culture: Youth justice in New Zealand.* Wellington: Social Policy Agency and Institute of Criminology

Millham, S, Bullock, R, Hosie, K, and Little, M (1986) *Lost in Care: The problems of maintaining links between children in care and their families.* Aldershot: Gower

Monk, DR (1996) *The Use of Genograms to Identify Intergenerational Child Abuse.* Unpublished M Phil thesis, University of Exeter

National Centre for Social Research (1999) *British Social Attitudes Survey.* Abingdon: Ashgate

Oliver, JE (1993) Intergenerational transmission of child abuse. *American Journal of Psychiatry,* **150**(9), 1315–24

Rowe, J, Cain, H, Hundleby, M, Keane, A (1984) *Long-term Foster Care.* London: Batsford/BAAF

Rowe, J, Hundleby, M, Garrett, L (1989) *Child Care Now: A survey of placement patterns.* London: BAAF

Rutter, M (1990) Psychosocial resilience and protection mechanisms. In J Rolf, et al (eds) *Risk and Protective Factors in the Development of Psychopathology,* pp181–214. Cambridge: Cambridge University Press

Rutter, M, Giller, H, Hagell, A (1998) *Antisocial Behaviour by Young People.* Cambridge: Cambridge University Press

Ryburn, M (1993) A new model for family decision making in child care and protection. *Early Child Development and Care,* **86**, 1–10

Ryburn, M and Atherton, C (1996) Family group conferences: partnership in practice. *Adoption and Fostering,* **20**, 16–23

Silverstein, M and Long, JD (1998) Trajectories of grandparents' perceived solidarity with adult grandchildren: a growth curve analysis over 23 years. *Journal of Marriage and the Family,* **60**, 912–23

Smith, G (1994) Parent, partner, protector: conflicting role demands for mothers of sexually abused children. In T Morrison, M Erooga, RC Beckett (eds) *Sexual Offending Against Children: Assessment and treatment of male abusers,* pp178–202. London: Routledge

Sonuga-Barke, E and Mistry, M (2000) The effect of extended family living on the mental health of three generations within two Asian communities. *British Journal of Clinical Psychology,* **39**, 129–41

Swain, P and Ban, P (1997) Participation and partnership – family group conferencing in the Australian context. *Journal of Social Welfare and Family Law,* **19**(1), 35–52

Thompson, RA (1995) *Preventing Child Maltreatment Through Social Support.* Thousand Oaks: Sage

Tietjen, AM (1989) The ecology of children's social support networks. In D Belle (ed) *Children's Social Networks and Social Supports,* pp37–69. New York: Wiley

Unger, D and Cooley, M (1992) Partner and grandmother contact in black and white teen parent families. *Journal of Adolescent Health*, **13**, 546–52

Uttal, L (1999) Using kin for child care: embedment in the socio-economic networks of extended families. *Journal of Marriage and the Family*, **61**, 845–57

Wellman, B and Wortley, S (1990) Different strokes from different folks: community ties and social support. *American Journal of Sociology*

Werner, E and Smith, R (1992) *Overcoming the Odds: High risk children from birth to adulthood*. Ithaca: Cornell University Press

Yabiku, ST, Axinn, WG, Thornton, A (1999) Family integration and children's self-esteem. *American Journal of Sociology*, **104**(5), 1494–524

Family history and functioning 8

It is important to point out that this chapter differs significantly from the other chapters in this volume. Whilst the other dimensions along the 'missing' side of the triangle are concerned with issues that are largely external to the family, the history and functioning of families is obviously concerned with what happens within them. In many ways, it might have been more logical to locate this dimension *within* the Assessment Framework triangle, rather than along one of its sides. However, the advantage of including this chapter alongside the other dimensions is that it provides an opportunity to examine the interactions between the internal and external worlds of the family, another important theme of the book.

The chapter begins with a consideration of some of the ways in which genetic factors and inherited characteristics can affect children and their families. It then looks at the various ways in which children's relationships with their immediate family members can influence their development and the sort of parents that they are likely to become in the future. Thirdly, we examine the main ways in which the personal characteristics and behaviour of adults, who are also parents, can influence their capacity to successfully look after their children. This is followed by consideration of some of the ways that the composition and structure of families can influence how they function. As in the chapters in the rest of this volume, we conclude with a summary of the most significant issues that have been identified for assessments

Inherited characteristics

At the outset of this section it is important to clarify that, whilst all children inherit certain traits and characteristics from their parents, the way that this influences the child's development is dependent on their subsequent experiences (Robins and Rutter, 1990). For example, whilst some mental illnesses have a genetic component, this usually acts only as a predisposing vulnerability, with the actual onset and maintenance of illness dependent on stressful life events and circumstances (Coyne and Downey, 1991). It is interesting to note, in this regard, that the stresses involved in parenthood for women in UK society, especially those living on low incomes, are considered to be largely responsible for the fact that the prevalence of depression amongst women in the general population is twice as high as that for men (Downey and Coyne, 1990; Brown and Harris, 1978). At any given time approximately 8 per cent of mothers are estimated to be clinically depressed, rising to 12 per cent in the post-natal period (O'Hara, 1986).

To date, upwards of 3,000 different diseases and conditions with a genetic component have been identified. These include autism, cystic fibrosis, Down's syndrome, muscular dystrophy, sickle-cell anaemia, and spina bifida, that are evident either before or soon after birth, or develop in early childhood. Many of these conditions are the result of apparently tiny differences in genetic make-up. Cystic fibrosis, for example, is caused by a single gene that was first identified in 1989. Although one person in every 22 is a carrier of the defective gene, it is only when two carriers have children that the risk becomes significant. Each child then has a one-in-four chance of inheriting the condition, leading to its occurrence in about one in every 2,000 pregnancies. Down's syndrome is also the result of a small genetic abnormality, involving the presence of an extra copy of chromosome 21 in every cell, which produces intellectual impairment as well as some characteristic physical features. It most commonly occurs in births to mothers over the age of 40, in whom 1 per cent of pregnancies are likely to result in a child with the syndrome (Curtis, 1986).

Overall, there are estimated to be some 360,000 children under the age of 16 with a significant disability in England and Wales, a prevalence rate of 32 per 1,000 of the child population (Department of Health, 2000a). However, when the much larger proportion of children who are affected by chronic illness is added to this figure, the prevalence rate rises to somewhere nearer to 150 per 1,000 of the child population (Eiser, 1993). The majority of these children will be suffering from conditions that have a genetic component, although many will also have an environmental component as well. Multiple disability is common and the vast majority of these children will be living at home with their parents (Social Services Inspectorate, 1998). It is almost impossible to overestimate the impact, for both the child and their family, of childhood disability or chronic illness. A recent review of UK research in this field highlights the problems faced by families in which there is a child with disabilities. The review emphasises the links with all the factors on the 'missing' side of the assessment triangle. Compared to families without disabled children, those with a disabled child are more likely to be living on low *incomes*, with diminished *employment* opportunities, in inadequate *housing*, and with poorer access to *community resources*, often being excluded from mainstream services (Joseph Rowntree Foundation, 1999). For example, parents were spending twice as much on their disabled children as parents of non-disabled children, but they still considered this to be insufficient to give their children a reasonable standard of living. As one parent commented:

'It's hard because you want to do more ... I spend what I have, sometimes I spend more than that. Me and her dad do without and we manage, but it's not easy for me or her. She knows we worry all the time about money and bills, so she doesn't ask for things.' (Dobson, Middleton and Beardsworth, 2001, pp2–3)

Minority ethnic families with a disabled child are particularly disadvantaged, tending to have lower *incomes*, less emotional and practical support from their *wider family*, and more likely to be living in unsuitable *housing* than their white counterparts (Chamba et al, 1999).

In addition to inherited conditions and diseases, there are also a wide range of physical and psychological traits that bear the hallmark of our parents' genes. For the most part these signs of inheritance are an important element of our personal identity and contribute a sense of belonging within biological family networks. However, for a significant minority of children and parents they may be a painful reminder of biological relationships with people who are no longer a part of their household, or who have behaved in ways that have been damaging or hurtful towards those who will forever share their genes. There are also about 10 per cent of infants who are born with what are termed 'difficult temperaments', being socially withdrawn, prone to crying, and generally difficult to satisfy, who present their carers with particular challenges and are at higher risk of developmental problems (Rutter, 1989; Thomas and Chess, 1982). The case of children born with difficult temperaments illustrates the point made at the beginning of this section about the interaction between inherited characteristics and subsequent environmental influences. The likelihood of difficult early temperament leading to later developmental problems is greatly increased when it occurs within the context of other family difficulties and wider environmental stresses (Prior, 1992). This is an issue that is also important in the next section, where we consider the impact of family relationships and home circumstances on children and the significance that these may have when they become parents.

The influence of family relationships and home circumstances

Historically, the research literature concerned with children's family relationships has placed a heavy emphasis on children's interactions with their mothers in the first few years of life. It is only in more recent years that significant attention has also been given to children's relationships over the duration of their whole childhood, with other family members (eg, fathers and siblings), and also to the influence of family members' relationships with each other on the developing child.

The preoccupation with children's early years is understandable when it is realised how important they are in laying the foundations for all later relationships. If it is the brain that 'makes us human' (Jones, 1999, p422), the rapid growth of the brain in the early years, reaching half of its final weight at 6 months and 90 per cent by 5 years of age, is obviously of huge significance for the sort of person that we are to become. The quality and nature of the child's early environment, especially the main relationships that the child has during this period, are therefore crucial in determining the way that the brain develops – the number, complexity, and structuring of the neuron connections formed: '…the 'driving' role of sensory input in organising neuronal development mean that a lack of the relevant experiences can have a lasting effect on brain development.' (Rutter and Rutter, 1992 p40)

The child's early relationships with their main carers are biologically driven by what John Bowlby described as 'attachment behaviour' on the part of the infant, designed to ensure that physical and emotional needs are met. The nature of these early stimuli shape the development and structure of the brain, which is growing in ways that best help the infant to make sense of the world. Bowlby developed the concept of 'inner working models' of relationships to describe this process, with these early cognitive structures then helping the child to understand subsequent experiences. In this way, it can be seen that an individual's perception of any given situation or relationship is unique to them and is also influenced by their previous history of experiences and relationships. This history will help to determine not only what is perceived, but also how it is most likely to be responded to, and whether or not similar experiences will be sought out, or avoided, in the future (Bowlby, 1973).

So, a child growing up in a family with parents or carers who are able to respond to them sensitively and to meet their needs in a reliable and satisfying way, is likely to develop coherent working models of relationships that provide a sound basis for future development. Stimulation and new experiences help the brain to develop, which integrates these new stimuli into its existing cognitive structures. Conversely, insensitive or unreliable care will tend to produce internal working models that are confused, fragmented or contradictory, providing an inadequate basis on which to accommodate subsequent experiences.

Mary Ainsworth (1973) was the first researcher to identify consistent patterns in the attachments young children developed, depending upon the parent's level of responsiveness. Children who had experienced satisfactory care developed what were called 'secure' attachments, whilst those who had experienced deficits in care displayed one of two different forms of 'insecure' attachment: 'avoidant', in response to repeated parental rejections, or 'ambivalent/resistant', as a result of inconsistent or chaotic care (Ainsworth et al, 1978). Subsequently, a third category of insecure attachment, termed 'disorganised', was added, usually associated with parental loss, abuse or severe neglect (Main, 1991). These different types of attachment security, the contexts within which they arise, and the consequences for children's development have been described in more detail in publications by David Howe and his colleagues at the University of East Anglia (Howe, 1995; Howe et al, 1999). Following a thorough review of the research evidence, Howe concludes that insecure attachments disturb children's ability 'to organise and model social experience, form a core concept of self, cope with anxiety, develop social understanding, make sense of other people, and cope with social relationships' (Howe, 1995, p97). For example, there is evidence that clearly links insecure attachment formation with abuse. In one study, over four out of five children who had experienced significant harm within their families displayed disorganised attachments, compared to less than one in five children in a non-abused control group (Carlson et al, 1989).

However, as already mentioned, the almost exclusive emphasis on attachment security between mother and child can be criticised for its failure to pay sufficient attention to other significant relationships (or facets of relationships) and environments affecting children's development, throughout their childhood. For example, there is evidence that suggests that father–child relationships have more of an influence over children's peer friendships than mother–child relationships (Dunn, 1993). The focus on mother–child attachment security also tends to over-emphasise the parent's influence on the child at the expense of a fuller consideration of the part played by the child's individual temperament and other characteristics (Dunn, 1993). As any parent knows, the relationships they form with different children in their family are crucially dependent upon the individual characteristics and subsequent experiences of the children themselves. It is often these differences in children's relationships with their parents, within the same family, that have the most marked impact on children's development, with effects that often last throughout the remainder of their lives (Dunn and Plomin, 1990; Sulloway, 1997).

The focus on family relationships can also distract attention from the important influence of the overall home environments to which children are exposed, at different ages and in different ethnic and economic contexts, on their development (Bradley et al, 2001a). For example, we know that, at younger ages, children are likely to receive both more physical affection and punishment from their parents. They are also likely to be read to more frequently at a younger age whereas, as they get older (up to early adolescence), they are increasingly likely to be taken to places of interest and group activities outside the home. However, parents experiencing the stress associated with poverty tend to display less affection towards their children and give harsher punishment. Poverty also reduces the chances that children will have meaningful contact with their fathers or experience developmentally stimulating environments. These effects of poverty are consistent across ethnic groups, although some ethnic group differences can be identified that reflect cultural and neighbourhood influences on children's development.

Variations in home environments like these are associated with a range of developmental outcomes for children. The level of stimulation of learning in the home environment of children of all ages is well known to influence early social and motor development, as well as later language competence, behaviour and achievement. Parental responsiveness in meeting young children's needs is also associated with the child's early social and motor development but other aspects of the home and wider social environments become more important for different areas of children's development as they grow older (Bradley et al, 2001b).

This concern, about the longer-term influences of early environments, somewhat paradoxically, brings us back to one of the major strengths of the attachment security concept. There is now considerable evidence of the tendency for attachment patterns, developed early in life, to continue into adult life, where they play a significant role in parenting (Caspi and

Elder, 1988; Reder and Duncan, 1999). For example, Crittenden (Crittenden, 1985) and Polansky and his colleagues (Polansky et al, 1985) have both demonstrated the way that the parenting deficits of abusing and neglecting parents represent more general problems with relationships that can be traced back to the formation of insecure early childhood attachments. Further support for the intergenerational continuity of attachment patterns is provided by Main and her colleagues (Main et al, 1985). They identified three different types of adult attachment patterns among parents (associated with the degree to which they had psychologically come to terms with their childhood relationships with their own parents) that were being replicated in the attachments of their own children. Here, the crucial factor was not so much the nature of the original relationships per se, but rather whether parents had subsequently resolved their feelings about these relationships. Those parents who either remained caught up in the feelings attached to the original relationship or who blocked out any unhappy memories associated with them, tended to be experiencing problems in the formation of secure attachment relationships with their own children.

This last point alerts us, once again, to the need to consider not only originating circumstances, but what happens subsequently. So, while there is good evidence to show, for example, the risk of 'transmission' of child abuse, from one generation to the next, this is far from inevitable. Positive later experiences and environments, such as supportive relationships with other significant people, either in childhood or adulthood, can produce more discontinuities than continuities in rates of transmission (Kaufman and Zigler, 1989). This interplay, between individual characteristics, interpersonal experiences, and environmental factors, therefore shapes parenting capacity and all other aspects of adult personality and behaviour (Vondra and Belsky, 1993). It is to some of these different aspects of personality and behaviour that we now turn, to consider the influence that they can have on the development of children.

Adult behaviour and characteristics

The child protection system that has developed in the UK is characterised by an emphasis on family and individual pathology, legal and administrative interventions, and professional responsibility (Jack, 1997). In this context, it is not surprising to find high levels of removals of children from families where adults have serious problems deemed to pose a threat to the safety and development of their children. For example, it has been estimated that somewhere between 40 and 60 per cent of children were removed from the families of parents with identified learning disabilities in the past 30 years of the twentieth century, in both the UK and the USA (Booth and Booth, 1998). Although more recent work has begun to challenge what the Booths refer to as the 'presumption of incompetence' (p2) that appears to have informed such practice, the UK government's own survey of local authority services for disabled parents reveals how much still remains to be achieved (Social Services Inspectorate, 2000).

A number of recent publications in the UK have considerably improved access to the evidence upon which to base more balanced assessments of the potential influence of specific adult problems – such as mental illness, substance misuse, and disability – on parenting capacity and child development (eg, Reder and Lucey, 1995; Cleaver, Unell and Aldgate, 1999). Overall, the messages emerging from the research indicate that, in most cases, with the availability of appropriate support, children can live in a family with a parent who has an isolated problem, such as a disability, or a mental illness, or a drug problem, without suffering significant harm (Cassell and Coleman, 1995; Coleman and Cassell, 1995; Gath, 1995; Brisby, Baker and Hedderwick, 1997). The crucial issues for assessments are the degree to which the parent's behaviour or condition actually interferes with the day-to-day tasks of parenting, the support available from other adults in the household and wider family members, the individual characteristics of their children, the economic and social circumstances in which they are living, and the community resources available to them from statutory and voluntary organisations and associations. In other words, there should be a full ecological assessment, taking into account the three domains of the Assessment Framework (Department of Health, 2000b), rather than an exclusive focus on the adult problem per se. It is when such individual adult problems are found in combination, either with each other, or with other serious problems in the family environment, such as parental conflict and domestic violence, that the risk of harm to children is significantly increased. As Hedy Cleaver and her colleagues conclude, 'when families remain cohesive and harmonious, the children generally grow up relatively unharmed' (Cleaver, Unell and Aldgate, 1999, p23). A large amount of research evidence points to the damaging consequences, for any child, of growing up in a family context in which parental conflict and domestic violence is a chronic problem. For example, families that initiate and reciprocate aggressive behaviours tend to produce children who are disruptive and aggressive themselves (Dadds, 1995). We now go on to consider this aspect of family functioning in more detail, as part of a wider examination of the influence of the membership and structure of different sorts of households on children's development.

Family composition and structure

In the UK, as elsewhere in the developed world, the second half of the twentieth century was a period of significant changes in the composition and structure of many families and households, leading to an increasing diversity of family forms and domestic arrangements. However, these changes have taken place within the context of considerable continuities in the patterns of domestic life within families (Allen and Crow, 2001). This mixture of change and continuity was nicely captured by Lorna Sage, in her recent memoir, in which she observed that:

'In the land of the 1950s you were meant to be socially mobile, but personally conformist; self-made, but in one of the moulds made ready. You mustn't miss the boat, but you mustn't rock it either.' (Sage, 2000, pp138–9)

The proportion of households with children headed by a lone parent, or consisting of parents with children from previous relationships, rose significantly during this period, although these changes vary according to such factors as ethnic origin. For example, analysis of the 1991 census reveals that 55 per cent of Caribbean families with children under the age of 16 were classified as lone parents, compared to only 8 per cent of Indian families. The analysis also found that a higher proportion of minority ethnic households consist of families with children than those of the white population (Haskey, 1997). In fact, attitudes towards a wide range of family issues, including lone parenthood, cohabitation, marriage, and child-rearing, vary significantly with ethnicity. Minority ethnic families differ in significant ways from white families, but also differ in a number of ways from each other (Beishon, Modood and Virdee, 1998).

With increasing levels of lone parenthood, family disruption and family re-constitution, many people have become concerned about the effects of these changes on children's development. This is a highly contested area, with the results of a whole range of research studies and media surveys often revealing more about the beliefs and attitudes of those funding or undertaking the 'research', than providing a reliable guide to any real effects on children. What is undoubtedly true, however, is that most children find the experience of their parents' separation to be both confusing and distressing (Dunn and Deater-Deckard, 2001). In part, this is due to the fact that so few children – only one in sixteen in one study – are prepared for it by satisfactory explanations from both parents (Cockett and Tripp, 1994).

Many of the effects on children of family breakdown, including unhappiness, low self-esteem, behaviour and peer relationship problems, and loss of contact with wider family members, tend to be fairly short term, diminishing over time for the majority of children. However, longer-term adverse effects remain for a minority of children. Repeated experiences of family breakdown and reconstitution have especially detrimental effects on children (Rodgers and Pryor, 1998; Cockett and Tripp, 1994). In general the effects of family disruptions on children appear to arise primarily from the changes in family composition and relationships involved, and the associated economic, social and psychological difficulties, rather than the resulting family structures and composition per se. This may be why children in lone-parent families are often found to be developing more satisfactorily than those who have experienced both family disruption and the readjustments involved in step-family formation. In step-families it has been found that both adults report more relationship difficulties and disagreements over child-rearing and children are less likely to have contact with the non-resident parent, than in lone-parent families (Ferri and Smith, 1998; Cockett and Tripp, 1994).

It is also important to point out, though, that many of the apparent 'effects' of family disruption on children are more a reflection of the circumstances that prevailed before the disruption occurred, or following it (Burghes, 1994). This applies especially to family conflict, which is known to have a damaging effect on many aspects of children's development and, in particular, is associated with an increased level of behaviour problems (Rodgers and Pryor, 1998). In fact, children growing up in families characterised by high levels of parental disharmony may even benefit from their parents' separation and divorce if this results in a reduction in parental conflict (Amato and Booth, 1997). What can be described as 'functional' families (whether intact or step-families) have been shown to share many similarities, including good marital adjustment, strong bonds between biological parents and children, the inclusion of all family members, and the ability to make mutual compromises in reaching family decisions. By contrast, 'dysfunctional' families (of both types) were found to be characterised by disruptive coalitions between biological parents and their children, and a lack of mutual decision-making

(Anderson and White, 1986). Overall, therefore, this study illustrates the similarities between families that are either functional or dysfunctional, regardless of their structure and composition.

Issues for assessment

In relation to a child's inherited characteristics, assessments will be attempting to identify the particular ways that a child's developmental needs, and the parenting that they require, are influenced by the environmental niche that the family occupies. We have already seen that families that have a child with a disability or a chronic illness are more likely to experience a wide range of disadvantages. These include the likelihood that they will have to live on a lower income, in more unsuitable accommodation, and with more restricted access to employment opportunities and mainstream community resources than other families. It was also noted that minority ethnic families with disabled children are at risk of experiencing even greater difficulties, often including more restricted social support networks. The effects of disadvantages like these, compounded by the psychological impact of a child's disability, on the child and other family members, and the extra demands involved in parenting a child with special needs, can stretch a family's coping resources to their limits (Eiser, 1993).

Assessments, in these situations, will be attempting to help the family to understand the way that various factors in their wider family and environmental circumstances are interacting with one another to increase the pressures on the family. Through this shared process of information gathering and analysis, it should be possible to begin to identify those aspects of the family's situation that might be improved by action focused on their external circumstances. For example, helping to improve the family's access to local education, childcare, and leisure services, perhaps involving advocacy on the family's behalf with other agencies and the use of family support workers, classroom assistants and volunteers, might be important, both for the child's development and to support the parents and other family members. Alternatively, the main priority might be maximising the family's income, addressing their housing situation, or improving the social support available to them within their wider family and friendship networks. These interventions are likely to involve close liaison with other agencies and professionals, as well as linking families into networks of people who have the capacity to provide supportive resources to the family or its individual members. Where such networks do not already exist, the task may involve helping to develop the capacity of local neighbourhoods to support families experiencing particular pressures (Jack and Jack, 2000).

Moving on to the influence of family relationships and the home environment, all work with children in need and their families will involve assessments of the quality of the child's relationships with their parents and carers, now and in the past. Again, what will be important in ecological assessment work is that the wider family and environmental context within which these relationships exist, or were developed, is understood and taken into consideration. Workers may be trying to establish, for example, whether any difficulties in the current parent–child relationship are linked to the attachment histories of the parents themselves. If they are, does the work of Main and her colleagues, described earlier in the chapter, give some pointers to the sort of therapeutic work that might need to be undertaken, with the parents, before they are able to interact more positively with their children? Arranging for a parent who has unresolved attachment problems of their own to attend a family centre or a parenting class is unlikely to be successful without some prior therapeutic work with them as an individual. Work of this kind may also be the key to improving the parent's social support resources, since unresolved attachment issues may be hindering the development or use they can make of their wider family and friendship networks. In addition to these sorts of issues, assessments of the quality of the home environment will need to take into account the effects of factors such as family *income, social integration, housing* and *community resources*, both on the family's current circumstances, and on the parents' development in their own childhood. This is where providing access to a range of community resources, such as childcare, parenting classes, family centres, toy libraries, and the support available from other parents or home visitors, may be part of the solution to improving the level of stimulation of learning that the child experiences.

When dealing with family situations in which the particular characteristics or behaviour of the adult members of the family are a concern, including mental illness, learning disability, and substance misuse, the assessment task involves identifying in what particular ways these adult issues are affecting their parenting capacity, or the child's development. The research evidence strongly suggests that this will depend, not only on the severity of the adult's problems, but also on the characteristics of the children in the family and the other factors along the 'missing' side of the Assessment

Framework triangle, such as *social integration* and *community resources*. The question, here, is to what extent the family's overall circumstances enable any individual parental problems to be adequately compensated for by the strengths that exist elsewhere? These strengths might lie in the presence of a competent and stable adult partner in the same household, or the availability of a supportive close relative or friend, or long-term residence in a community with good quality services, or in which neighbours are used to supporting the family at times of need. Where these strengths are absent, workers will need to turn their attentions to devising interventions that aim to provide them, perhaps through efforts to enhance the social support available to the family in their local area, as well as facilitating access to specialist services, if appropriate.

However, the research evidence also highlights the damaging effects for children's development of chronic or serious parental conflict, or domestic violence. Where significant and long-term conflict exists between parents or carers, the outcomes for children are likely to be poor unless the level of disharmony can be effectively reduced, no matter what the other environmental circumstances of the family. It is important that assessments recognise situations in which domestic violence or serious conflict between parents and carers exists and that they target the resolution of these problems in any plans that are agreed with the family. However, it is also important that these plans are informed by an awareness of the way that such conflict might be affected by the family's wider family and environmental circumstances. In most cases it is likely that a combination of individual characteristics and pressures elsewhere, in the family's external circumstances, are responsible for either triggering or sustaining the conflict that exists between the adults in the family. In its own turn, such internal family conflict is likely to influence the family's external circumstances, perhaps leading to the temporary loss of accommodation, social isolation, and reductions in income, providing a powerful illustration of the interdependence of different factors found within the ecological model.

What research is also able to tell us is that family composition and structure, per se, tend to be less important for most children's development than the effects of parental conflict. Families can function well, whether they are intact, nuclear-type families with two parents, or reconstituted step-parent families, or single-parent families. What is important for family functioning appears to be similar, no matter what the particular composition of the family, and assessments therefore need to focus on a family's particular strengths and vulnerabilities, rather than its structure or membership in isolation. However, repeated experiences of family disruption and reformation, or unresolved feelings from past experiences and losses, should be identified in assessments because these issues are likely to be the cause of ongoing problems for children's emotional and behavioural development. Also, differences in family structures and membership are, to some extent, likely to be a reflection of variations in attitudes towards a wide range of family issues. Different attitudes in relation to lone parenthood, cohabitation, marriage, divorce and the norms of child-rearing, all of which are likely to vary according to such factors as social class, culture and religion, may influence children's development and choices in later life and, as such, may be relevant to include in assessments.

References

Ainsworth, M (1973) The development of infant-mother attachment. In BM Caldwell and HN Riecuiti (eds) *Review of Child Development*, Vol 3. Chicago: Chicago University Press

Ainsworth, M, Blehar M, Waters, E, Wall, S (1978) *Patterns of Attachment: A psychological study of the strange situation*. Hillsdale, NJ: Erlbaum

Allan, G and Crow, G (2001) *Families, Households and Society*. Basingstoke: Palgrave

Amato, PR and Booth, A (1997) A generation at risk: growing up in an era of family upheaval. In *Research Matters 'Families'* (F McGlone), Oct.1998 – Apr. 1999 (pp6–8)

Anderson, JZ and White, GD (1986) An empirical investigation of interaction and relationship patterns in functional and dysfunctional nuclear families and stepfamilies. *Family Process*, **25**, 407–21

Beishon, S, Modood, T, Virdee, S (1998) *Ethnic Minority Families*. London: Policy Studies Institute

Booth, T and Booth, W (1998) *Growing Up with Parents Who Have Learning Difficulties*. London: Routledge

Bowlby, J (1973) *Attachment and Loss: Vol.2: Separation: Anxiety and anger*. London: Hogarth

Bradley, RH, Corwyn, RF, McAdoo, HP, Coll, CG (2001a) The home environments of children in the United States. Part I: Variations by age, ethnicity, and poverty status. *Child Development*, **72**(6), 1844–67

Bradley, RH, Corwyn, RF, Burchinal, M, McAdoo, HP, Coll, CG (2001b) The home environments of children in the United States. Part II: Relations with behavioural development through age thirteen. *Child Development*, **72**(6), 1868–86

Brisby, T, Baker, S, Hedderwick, T (1997) *Under the Influence: Coping with parents who drink too much.* London: Alcohol Concern

Brown, GW and Harris, T (1978) *Social Origins of Depression.* London: Tavistock

Burghes, L (1994) *Lone Parenthood and Family Disruption: The outcomes for children.* London: Family Policy Studies Centre

Carlson, V, Cicchetti, D, Barnett, D, Braunwald, K (1989) Disorganised/ disoriented attachment relationships in maltreatment infants. *Developmental Psychology,* **25**, 525–31

Caspi, A and Elder, GH (1988) Emergent family patterns: the intergenerational construction of problem behaviour and relationships. In RA Hinde and J Stevenson-Hinde (eds) *Relationships Within Families: Mutual influences,* pp218–40. Oxford: Clarendon

Cassell, D and Coleman, R (1995) Parents with psychiatric problems. In P Reder and C Lucey (eds) *Assessment of Parenting: Psychiatric and psychological contributions,* pp169–81. London: Routledge

Chamba, R, Ahmad, W, Hirst, M, Lawton, D, Beresford, B (1999) *On the Edge: Minority ethnic families caring for a severely disabled child.* Bristol: The Policy Press

Cleaver, H, Unell, I, Aldgate, J (1999) *Children's Needs – Parenting Capacity: The impact of parental mental illness, problem alcohol and drug use, and domestic violence on children's development.* London: The Stationery Office

Cockett, M and Tripp, J (1994) *The Exeter Family Study: Family breakdown and its impact on children.* Exeter: Exeter University Press

Coleman, R and Cassell, D (1995) Parents who misuse drugs and alcohol. In P Reder and C Lucey (eds) *Assessment of Parenting: Psychiatric and psychological contributions,* pp182–93. London: Routledge

Coyne, JC and Downey, G (1991) Social factors and psychopathology: stress, social support and coping processes. *Annual Review of Psychology,* **42**, 401–25

Crittenden, PM (1985) Social networks, quality of child rearing and child development. *Child Development,* **56**, 1299–313

Curtis, S (ed) (1986) *From Asthma to Thalassaemia: Medical conditions in childhood.* London: BAAF

Dadds, MR (1995) *Families, Children, and the Development of Dysfunction.* Thousand Oaks, California: Sage

Department of Health (2000a) *Children Act Report 1995–1999.* London: The Stationery Office

Department of Health (2000b) *Framework for the Assessment of Children in Need and their Families.* London: The Stationery Office

Dobson, B, Middleton, S, Beardsworth, A (2001) *The Impact of Childhood Disability on Family Life.* York: York Publishing Services

Downey, G and Coyne, JC (1990) Children of depressed parents: an integrative review. *Psychological Bulletin*, **108**, 5–76

Dunn, J (1993) *Young Children's Close Relationships: Beyond attachment*. Newbury Park, California: Sage

Dunn, J and Deater-Deckard, K (2001) *Children's Views of their Changing Families*. York: York Publishing Services

Dunn, J and Plomin, R (1990) *Separate Lives: Why siblings are so different*. New York: Basic Books

Eiser, C (1993) *Growing Up with a Chronic Disease: The impact on children and their families*. London: Jessica Kingsley

Ferri, E and Smith, K (1998) *Step-Parenting in the 1990s*. London: Family Policy Studies Centre

Gath, A (1995) Parents with learning disability. In P Reder and C Lucey (eds) *Assessment of Parenting: Psychiatric and psychological contributions*, pp194–203. London: Routledge

Haskey, J (1997) *Population Review (8). The ethnic minority and overseas-born population of great Britain, Populations Trends No. 88*. London: Office of National Statistics

Howe, D (1995) *Attachment Theory for Social Work Practice*. Basingstoke: Macmillan

Howe, D, Brandon, M, Hinings, D, Schofield, G (1999) *Attachment Theory, Child Maltreatment and Family Support*. Basingstoke: Macmillan

Jack, G (1997) Discourses of child protection and child welfare. *British Journal of Social Work*, **27**, 659–78

Jack, G and Jack, D (2000) Ecological social work: the application of a systems model of development in context. In P Stepney and D Ford (eds) *Social Work Models, Methods and Theories: A framework for practice*, pp93–104. Lyme Regis: Russell House

Jones, S (1999) *Almost Like a Whale*. London: Transworld/Anchor

Joseph Rowntree Foundation (1999) *Foundations: Supporting disabled children and their families*. York: JRF

Kaufman, J and Zigler, E (1989) The intergenerational transmission of child abuse and the prospect of predicting future abusers. In D Cicchetti and V Carlson (eds) *Child Maltreatment: Research and theory on the consequences of child abuse and neglect*, pp129–50. Cambridge, MA: Harvard University Press

Main, M (1991) Metacognitive knowledge, metacognitive monitoring, and singular (coherent) vs. multiple (incoherent) model of attachment. In CM Parkes, J Stevenson-Hinde, and P Marris (eds) *Attachment Across the Life Cycle*. London: Routledge

O'Hara, M (1986) Social support, life events, and depression during pregnancy and the puererium. *Archives of General Psychiatry*, **43**, 569–73

Polansky, NA, Gaudin, JM, Ammons, PW, David, KB (1985) The psychological ecology of the neglectful mother. *Child Abuse and Neglect*, **9**, 265–75

Prior, M (1992) Childhood temperament. *Journal of Child Psychology and Psychiatry*, **33**(1), 249–79

Reder, P and Duncan, S (1999) *Lost Innocents*. London: Routledge

Reder, P and Lucey, C (1995) *Assessment of Parenting: Psychiatric and psychological contributions*. London: Routledge

Robins, LN and Rutter, M (eds) (1990) *Straight and Devious Pathways from Childhood to Adulthood*. Cambridge: Cambridge University Press

Rodgers, B and Pryor, J (1998) *Divorce and Separation: The outcomes for children*. York: Joseph Rowntree Foundation

Rutter, M (1989) Pathways from childhood to adult life. *Journal of Child Psychology and Psychiatry*, **30**, 23–51

Rutter, NM and Rutter, M (1992) *Developing Minds: Challenge and continuity across the life span*. Harmondsworth: Penguin

Sage, L (2000) *Bad Blood*. London: Fourth Estate

Social Services Inspectorate (1998) *Disabled Children: Directions for their future care*. London: Department of Health

Social Services Inspectorate (2000) *A Jigsaw of Services: Inspection of services to support disabled adults in their parenting role*. London: Department of Health

Sulloway, FJ (1997) *Born to Rebel: Birth order, family dynamics and creative lives*. New York: Vintage Books

Thomas, A and Chess, S (1982) Temperament and follow-up to adulthood. In R Porter and GM Collins (eds) *Temperamental Differences in Infants and Young Children*, pp168–75. London: Pitman / Ciba Foundation

Vondra, J and Belsky, J (1993) Developmental origins of parenting: personality and relationship factors. In T Luster and L Okagaki (eds) *Parenting: An ecological perspective*, pp149–78. Hillsdale, NJ: Erlbaum

Implementing the framework 9

In this book we have considered the relationship between the internal and external experiences of the family. Assessments need to analyse the strengths and pressures that families experience, moving between factors inside the family and factors in their wider family networks and environmental circumstances.

In adopting this approach the Assessment Framework is consistent with other government initiatives in relation to children. Both the Children's Fund and Sure Start, as we said in the first chapter, have community involvement and community provision and their impact on children at their heart.

Implementation of the Assessment Framework does, however, need to be accompanied by major shifts in professional culture and practice, resource allocation, and organisational structures in UK child welfare. So far, agencies and practitioners have largely failed to respond to the need for such a paradigm shift and have merely switched to using another set of forms; these forms are larger and more comprehensive than previous forms, but their use needs to be accompanied by significant shifts in the way they operate. The danger of merely incorporating new forms into existing structures has been noted by Jordan who, whilst acknowledging that the Assessment Framework is '… admirably broad in scope, and it directs assessors to think about much wider factors in the lives of children and how to support their families…', nevertheless goes on to express concern about it becoming '…yet another assessment, another instrument for categorising people and fitting them into pre-existing boxes that correspond to [pre-existing] structures and policy imperatives…' (Jordan, 2001).

It is hardly surprising to find that the Assessment Framework has simply been incorporated into existing structures and practices in most agencies when the context in which it has been introduced is considered. A vast range of new central government targets and other policy initiatives in the childcare field have created unprecedented pressures on staff. Many of these initiatives, such as the requirement to undertake training for the post-qualifying childcare award, have also had the effect of reducing staffing levels in many organisations almost to breaking point.

The problem has been compounded by the government's failure to provide practitioners with the information or the tools required to integrate an understanding of the interactions between factors on all three sides of the triangle into their assessments.

It is also important to be realistic about the extent of change that can be achieved by individual workers and their employing organisations. This is a point that has already been made by a number of other commentators, including Parton, who has argued, in relation to new orientations towards family support, that it is important '… not simply to assume that all that is required is a change in front-line professionals' attitudes, re-labelling procedures and minor modifications to operational perspectives and practices. We may be in danger of expecting social workers and social services departments to resolve problems that are well beyond their remit and responsibility' (Parton, 1997, p11).

Housing, for instance, is one of the assessment categories on the bottom side of the triangle and we have shown how housing provision may impact on networks, access to community resources and social integration. But there is a long-standing crisis in the provision of social housing in the UK. Many rural and urban areas have long waiting lists of families who have no accommodation, or who are dissatisfied with their accommodation because it is inadequate for their needs or is in threatening neighbourhoods. The pressure that these families experience, which in turn produces stressed parenting, is the result of national and local policies and inadequate housing finances. We show below that partnership interventions in which social workers are involved, *can* have an impact but it is also essential not to obscure the wider policy and resource implications.

Bearing in mind these constraints, we look at some of the challenges that need to be addressed and changes that need to be made if the Assessment Framework and its ideal of an ecological approach to the welfare of children in need are to be incorporated into UK family support and child welfare work.

The challenge for research – developing new information about child and family welfare

At various points in this book we have noted the limited amount of UK research information available on the impact of external pressures on the internal dynamics of family life.

The picture is a very uneven one. In some areas, such as the impact of income deprivation and homelessness on children's lives, we now have good research which can guide assessments and subsequent interventions. In other areas, such as the cumulative impact on family life of living in poorly resourced, demographically unbalanced and threatening neighbourhoods, we have much less information. Furthermore, we know very little about what makes particular families resilient to these pressures and what makes others succumb.

Equally we have little UK research information on the significance of community networks in protecting children from significant harm and supporting parents. Although it is a complex area of inquiry, US research over the last 25 years has consistently pointed to aspects of isolation that are related to child mistreatment. The generation of this information and research base is particularly important if agencies are to move towards more community-based ways of working with children and parents.

Also we have little research information on the particular issues faced by different groups of children in different communities.

The Assessment Framework, and the new ways of thinking that underpin it, clearly challenge researchers to be directing their attention towards the connections between the internal and external worlds of families under pressure. This is not, however, a challenge only for researchers. Practitioners also need to build up a body of case histories which explore links between what happens within families and what happens in local neighbourhoods. The lessons from such case histories need to be incorporated into the way we think about child and family welfare (see Gill, Jones and Lewis, 2002).

The challenge for welfare agencies

Resource implications

There are clearly resource implications if the approach advocated in the Assessment Framework is to become part of the way in which agencies operate, in terms of both assessments and interventions. At one level, new resources will be needed to develop community provision for parents and children. The evidence is that this should be very locally based provision which is linked to the needs of specific groups of parents. More than ten years ago Gibbons concluded, from her research on family support and prevention, that 'parents under stress more easily overcome family problems….where there are many sources of family support available in local communities.'(Gibbons, 1990, p162).

Provision for children also needs to be very locally based and needs to be clearly linked with initiatives run and supported by local communities. This is an approach that has been consistently advocated by Holman, based on many years' experience of work on estates in the West Country and Glasgow. Holman (2002) sees a key way of protecting children as being 'financial backing for locally run community groups. Their members are the ones most likely to be in touch with vulnerable children.'

At another level the ecological approach to working with children and parents demands extra resources in terms of worker time. It takes time to develop information about community strengths and resources and to work with families to increase their support.

Links with local communities

Agency recognition of the importance of community strengths and support and the incorporation of these factors into work with families necessitates new ways of working in partnership with local people. This will involve identifying strength in local communities and supporting the development of community organisations. It will also involve allowing local communities to influence the ways in which agencies work.

These changes are not confined to social services departments. Recent work by the King's Fund (2001), for instance, has illustrated the changes necessary if health authorities are to respond more effectively to community needs. They concluded 'It is clear that radical organisational change is needed if working with communities is to become integral to the way that statutory sector organisations function.' They argued that, for long-term change to occur in this respect, organisations need to:

- manage conflict more constructively
- develop more sophisticated skills and techniques for engaging with communities
- change the dominant professional cultures within their organisation
- develop a more participatory culture through encouraging innovation and risk-taking.

Developing new ways of working in partnership with other agencies

Various agencies, including those responsible for housing, policing, planning, leisure services, and neighbourhood regeneration, play a crucial role in influencing the quality and nature of family environments. It is therefore important that strong partnerships and alliances should be developed between these agencies and others more directly responsible for child welfare, such as social services, education, health, and various voluntary organisations, for the benefit of supporting families. Such local partnerships and alliances allow agencies to look beyond individual referrals to recognise the pressures evident in particular areas and the collective experiences of groups of children and families. The following practice examples illustrate the way in which this more collective and collaborative approach, focusing on groups and localities, can be used to improve the circumstances of individual children and families.

Based on information from individual casework, social services and family centre managers became increasingly aware of the pressures experienced by young families in the local tower blocks. There was a mass of case evidence of the pressure that living in the high-rise blocks placed on parents. There was, for instance, case evidence of a parent tethering a child to furniture because of fear of the child getting onto the balcony. It was decided to carry out a straightforward exercise of counting the number of children living in the blocks and analysing where they lived.

> On the basis of the information collected, a local working group, comprising representatives from housing, health, and social services was set up. Over a period of time this group achieved better local understanding of the needs of children in the blocks. One result of this was the development of improved communal play facilities for children and increased opportunities for parents to meet together in groups. Policy initiatives were also developed to cut down the number of 'high-rise under-5s'. The overall environment for many children was improved and specific difficulties for individual families were also addressed.

> Local agencies became increasingly aware, through individual casework, of the impact of high rates of racial harassment targeted against black, minority ethnic and dual-heritage children in one local area. A racial harassment forum was set up consisting of social services, health, police, and housing. The benefits of this approach were both individual, in terms of the welfare of specific children and families, and also more general and long-term, leading to improvements for specific groups of families and the area in general. At the level of individual families the forum led to the sharing of case material, support for specific children and families, co-ordinated responses from the police in taking action against the perpetrators of harassment, and quicker rehousing options for individual families, where this was appropriate. In the long term, it led to improvements in police procedures and response times. It also led, ultimately, to a race equality project that became actively involved in work with local schools.

Both of these initiatives were based on the development of local partnerships between agencies that were initiated because of concerns that first emerged through individual casework with families. The challenge lies in recognising and responding appropriately when apparently individual problems represent wider collective concerns. The improvements that were achieved would not have been possible if these cases had continued to be dealt with on an individual basis.

Acknowledging the family's own definitions of their difficulties

We have referred to the importance of acknowledging children's and parents' own definitions of their strengths and difficulties. Interventions based on the ecological perspective need to incorporate these definitions in the formulation of what is needed to make a positive difference in children's and parents' lives and what would be most likely to work in a particular locality or with a particular family. Whilst there will be many situations in which the agency will also need to stand back from the evidence and ideas that the family is providing, nonetheless the new framework does offer a chance of joining more with parents in their definitions and, in so doing, helping empower them. If parents have repeatedly been told that the answer to their difficulties lies in their own family relationships and personal inadequacies then, to be included in an approach that fully incorporates an awareness of wider influences on these factors can be experienced as particularly empowering. To have their interpretations of the significance of housing, income and community factors validated by agencies may prove to be a powerful strengthening factor.

Challenges to workers

Being familiar with community strengths and networks

In Chapter 3 above on social integration we drew attention to the significance of networks of support for the welfare of families and children. If social workers and others involved in working directly with families are familiar with the communities in which they are working, there are real possibilities that the ecological perspective can lead to positive benefits for families.

Ecological assessments and interventions involve developing a clear understanding of the strengths and pressures that exist within particular locations. As we have shown, these strengths can include a culture of acceptance and the potential for reciprocity, local sources of organised support (eg groups, community organisations), and people who 'look out for' other people's children.

Equally, it is important that workers become familiar with the pressures that exist in local neighbourhoods and communities for parents and children, such as a lack of social integration, perhaps evident in a culture of 'keeping oneself to oneself', based on fears of exploitation or personal risk.

Ways of working with families

If the significance of networks for supporting parents and protecting children is accepted, and if the family's access to resources is regarded as important, then new ways of working face to face with families need to be developed. These will include: working with families to identify networks and resources in their local area; identifying and working with the personal resources and skills that families have in accessing resources; identifying the personal constraints on families to access resources. Some family members may lack the skill or confidence to develop helpful relationships with others and this needs to be incorporated into the work which is undertaken.

We do not underestimate the difficulties involved in this type of work – some of the most hard-pressed families are also those who most alienate others. However, developing the capacity of families to access resources and support can provide rich benefits to children and parents.

Professional culture and style of working

Adopting a wider and more community-based orientation can also have implications for the sense of security and identity of individual workers. In our experience, the majority of childcare workers say that they support the move towards a more ecological form of practice, and that it is the structures and priorities of their employing organisations that prevent them from doing this. However, there is little doubt that, for some workers, this way of working may not be consistent with their desire for professional status, autonomy and identity. The ecological approach inevitably involves working with a range of 'non-professional' people in local communities. This collaborative way of working, with small groups, with individuals, and with neighbourhood networks, may appear to be low key and unlikely to heighten the worker's sense of professional status. Also, working alongside community members may often appear to involve a 'commonsense' way of tackling difficulties. It will involve shared definitions with local resource providers and community members which may serve to undermine the individual worker's sense of being a professional with specific areas of expertise and knowledge.

These barriers to change have also been highlighted by Jordan, who has commented that '...despite protestations to the contrary, many social workers have a stake in a style of work which is power-laden, formal and individualised and some fear of a transition to approaches that involve greater sharing in groups and more negotiated, informal work.' (Jordan, 1997, p97).

Whilst we acknowledge these issues, we hope to have demonstrated that the claim to professional status does not need to be undermined by practice that is based on an ecological approach. If the foregoing chapters have demonstrated anything, it is surely that this approach is based on an extensive body of often complex knowledge, that requires both sophisticated analytical skills, in the formulation of assessments, and a wide range of interpersonal, networking, and organisational skills to put the outcomes of those assessments into action that benefits the children, families, and communities involved.

Conclusion

Despite the many barriers that undoubtedly stand in the way of successfully developing and implementing policies and practice that embody the ecological principles on which the Assessment Framework is founded, there are also some grounds for optimism. In addition to the enthusiasm of many workers for the approach, there are many examples of a wider environmental perspective being incorporated into practice with children and families. These include: the development of various support groups in local communities; involvement with local child and family anti-poverty measures; influencing housing allocations; developing communal play facilities for children, and engagement with initiatives designed to strengthen social cohesion in local areas by welcoming new families to the neighbourhood.

Whilst major changes in professional and organisational culture need the support of a clear political commitment, and sufficient time and resources to enable them to develop, the new Assessment Framework also fits well with other government initiatives to tackle social exclusion. The fact that the social inclusion agenda is in part driven by wider economic imperatives, designed to increase the competitiveness of the nation in an increasingly globalised economy, suggests that it is unlikely to disappear from the political landscape. We hope that this volume will play a part in the development of ecological practice which will incorporate a better understanding of the role that wider family and environmental factors play in the lives of children and their families.

References

Department of Health (1999) *Health Services Directorate*. Surestart. London

Gibbons, J (1990) *Family Support and Prevention: Studies in local areas*. London: HMSO

Gill, O, Jones, T, Lewis, J (2002) Children in the round. *Community Care* April 18–24

Holman, B (2002) Letter to *Guardian*, 4 September

Jordan, B (1997) in Parton (1997), as below

Jordan, B (2001) Family support: recent trends in social policy. *Respecting Children*, **14**(4), 241–51

King's Fund (2001) *Strategic Action Programme For Healthy Communities. Draft Key Points* 1–5. London: King's Fund

Parton, N (ed) (1997) *Child Protection and Family Support*. London: Routledge

Appendix

Areas for assessment in relation to the impact of family and environmental factors on the lives of children

This appendix gathers together the research evidence and practice experience discussed in this book to suggest key areas for assessment in each of the categories on the 'family and environmental factors' side of the triangle.

In keeping with the ecological approach we present these areas as an invitation for the analysis of individual family circumstances rather than as a checklist of questions to be asked in all circumstances.

Community resources

General perceptions (children and parents)

- The geographical area or community of interest that the child and parents draw their support from. Distinguish from agency definitions of 'community' which will be based on administrative boundaries

- The child's and parents' perception of their community. Distinguish between mother's and father's perception of 'community'

Community resources for parents

- Formal sources of support in the local area for parents (eg, counselling, advice services). Differences in availability for mothers and fathers

- Semi-formal sources of support (eg, parenting programmes, lone parents' groups). Differences in availability for mothers and fathers

- Informal sources of support (eg, drop-ins, community centres). Differences in availability for mothers and fathers
- The level of advice available about financial and practical matters (eg, advice centres)
- Anti-poverty initiatives available locally (eg, food co-operatives, credit unions)
- Level of childcare provision available locally. Whether this matches the parent's needs and resources (eg location, timing, cost, perceived quality)
- Parent's perception of accessibility of local community resources. (eg, issues of availability, geographical proximity, transport, cost, stigma, degree of welcome. Also particular issues of accessibility in relation to ethnic background, disability)
- Aspects of the parent's personal history and characteristics which might influence their ability to access local community resources (eg, depression, disabilities, low self-esteem, lack of self confidence in social settings, inability to express difficulties and support needs, experience of victimisation)

Community resources for children

- Quality of educational provision and social inclusiveness of local schools
- Level of formal support available for children (eg, counselling services, therapy groups)
- Level of semi-formal support available for children (eg, groups for specific children)
- Level of informal support available for children (eg, clubs, open-access leisure and recreational activities)
- Neighbourhood play provision available
- Level of anti-poverty provision available (eg, organised outings, group holidays)
- Whether local resources are appropriate for the specific age of the child
- Children's perception of community resources as accessible to them (eg, availability, geographical proximity, transport, cost, stigma, degree of welcome, particular issues of accessibility in relation to ethnic background and disability)

- Aspects of the child's personal history and characteristics which might influence their access to particular community resources (eg, experiences of bullying, racial harassment, neglect or abuse, disability or illness, the child's developing social skills in accessing resources)

Safety (children and parents)

- The child's and parents' perception of their 'community' as a safe one (including issues of physical safety, people safety, and drugs safety)
- Protective factors in the community as well as dangers

Social integration

Parent's social integration

- Potential support from outside the family
- Parent's ability to access this support
- Nature and quality of this support
- Extent of positive community norms around parenting
- Extent to which people in the neighbourhood 'watch out' for other people's children
- Family's history of residential mobility. The extent to which this has impacted on the family's ability to access network and neighbourhood support

For assessment purposes it may also be important to be specific about the nature and content of informal support. Gibbons' research work from the early 1990s (see Gill et al, 2000) provides a useful tool for these purposes. Her categorisation of the different aspects of social support and practical help incorporates the advice that may be given by community or neighbourhood members or wider family members. The aspects of social support that Gibbons identified were:

- advice about children
- relationship advice

- financial advice
- material help
- general help with children
- help with children in a crisis
- help with private feelings.

The child's social integration

School

- Continuity of schooling
- The child's relations with teachers
- Friendships at school and the relationship between these friendships and neighbourhood friendships
- Extent of the child's experience of bullying or harassment at school

Peer group and neighbourhood

- Extent of close friendships within the peer group
- Level of acceptance or rejection of the child by her or his peers
- The child's perception of the level of acceptance or rejection of the child by her or his peers
- The norms of behaviour of the peer group
- Issues of bullying or harassment in the neighbourhood
- Extent of positive contact with adults in the neighbourhood. Does the child feel safe in the neighbourhood?
- The child's involvement in activities in the neighbourhood (clubs, etc) that bring contact with other children
- Other adults in the wider family or neighbourhood who the child can go to if she/he is in difficulty or trouble
- The child's experience of residential mobility. The impact of residential mobility on the child's sense of social integration

Income

Level of income

- Information about all sources of income (and advice about how to maximise this, if appropriate)

Levels of debt

- Establish levels of debt repayments and duration of loan periods (what does this leave the family to live on?)
- Consider penalties incurred for late or non-payment (advocate or negotiate repayments to an affordable level, if possible)

Identification of vulnerable groups

- Families with young children (we know that young children's development is particularly sensitive to experiences of poverty)
- Lone-parent families, or families with three or more children
- Minority-ethnic families, especially those of Pakistani and Bangladeshi origin
- Parents and/or children with disabilities or chronic illnesses
- Reconstituted families where parents also carry financial responsibility for children in other households

Effects of poverty

- Experience of poverty is particularly damaging for parenting capacity and child development if it is either persistent, or permanent
- Effects of poverty on the physical quality of the home environment
- Poverty's influence on children's full participation in school, social networks, activities, and the quality of their diet

Personal perceptions of poverty

- Ascertain individual meaning and responses (these are likely to vary according to such factors as age, gender and culture)

Wider family support

- Can be an important source of resilience if parents or other relatives outside the home provide advice, emotional support, or practical help (eg, loans, gifts, treats, holidays, childcare, transport)
- Geographical location may be an important factor in maintaining regular contact and support

Social and environmental context

- Availability, quality and accessibility of community resources (childcare, schools, shops, youth clubs, adult education, leisure services)
- Access to advice services
- Geographical location in relation to accessing community resources (extra transport costs incurred)
- Safety of local environment for children (lack of income restricts families to their local areas)

Employment

Personal meaning

- Working (or not) and the type of work will carry different meanings for different people, depending on such factors as age, education, family background, culture and personal identity
- Degree of personal choice in employment status and security of arrangements

Parenting capacity

- Influence of employment status on such things as parents' availability for children and childcare, personal health, skills, knowledge, and social integration
- Links to availability of reliable and suitable childcare (costs, accessibility, quality, hours)

Individual history/characteristics

- Effects of parents' previous history/childhood on their employability
- Potential for enhancing the education and training of parents, to improve their employment prospects or earnings
- Disability or chronic illness (parents or children) – effects on employment opportunities and earning potential

Structural factors

- The influence of factors such as geographical location, gender, ethnicity and social class on employment

Housing

Suitability of accommodation

- Extent of overcrowding
- Access to outdoor play space
- Particular physical difficulties for parents in this accommodation (for instance carrying buggies up flights of stairs)
- Adequacy of housing for disabled children

Safety and health issues

- A healthy environment for children and their parents (considering eg, dampness, ventilation, heating, kitchen hygiene)
- Kitchen safety (eg, cooking areas and electrical appliances)
- Stairs and floors and windows safety (eg, stairgates in use, badly worn floor coverings, furniture dangerously close to windows)
- Specific safety issues for disabled children

People living nearby

- Difficulties with neighbours
- The child's experience of the immediate location of the accommodation
- Particular issues of race and racial harassment associated with the immediate location of the accommodation

Housing and networks

- The effect of location of the family's accommodation on the parent's social support networks
- The effect of location of the family's accommodation on children's networks
- Whether people in the immediate locality are supportive and protective of children

Housing location and access to services

- Closeness to the goods and services that the family needs
- Impact of where the family live on the children's participation in activities and clubs that are important for their social networks (including participation issues for black, other minority ethnic and dual-heritage children)
- The impact of housing location on access to services for disabled children

Housing and finances

- Impact of housing costs on family's financial position
- Debts associated with setting up home

Homelessness

- Impact of homelessness on the parents' formal and informal sources of help
- Impact of homelessness on the children's networks and sense of security

Education links

- Does the family's housing position affect access to education?
- Does the family's housing position affect stability of children's education experience?

Wider family

Parents' networks

- Family members providing advice and support (and frequency of contact) that enhance parenting capacity
- Significant deficits (eg, no grandparental figures)
- Conflictual relationships
- Burdensome relationships with significant members of wider family – that are more sources of pressure than support
- In three-generation households – balance of positive and negative effects on parents and children

Children's networks

- Influence of wider family relationships on children's development (identity, values, beliefs, sense of belonging, safety and behaviour)
- Presence (or absence) of close and significant relationship with one or more relatives (may need to be protected/supported as a source of resilience for children living in adverse circumstances)
- Involvement of most significant family members in reaching important decisions about children in need (family group meetings approach)

'Looked-after' children

- Exploration of all appropriate kinship care options – with local authority support (especially financial)
- Arrangements to promote children's contacts with all appropriate members of their wider family network

Family history and functioning

Inherited characteristics

- Implications of genetic inheritance for the child (disability, chronic illness, temperament, future vulnerabilities)
- Interactions between disability/chronic illness and wider environmental factors (such as income, housing, community resources and employment) or ethnicity

Family relationships

- Nature and quality of child's relationships with parents/carers, siblings and other relatives (including attachment patterns)
- Links between current parent–child relationship difficulties and parents' own history of attachments

Home environment

- Quality of home environment, in terms of such things as learning stimulation, parental responsiveness, levels of supervision and safety

Adult characteristics and behaviour

- Specific impact of any adult problems (eg, substance misuse, mental health, disability) on parenting capacity and child's development
- Presence or absence of protective factors, such as supportive relatives or neighbours, when adult problems exist
- Parental disharmony, domestic violence, or history of violence or serious/persistent criminality in adult's background

Family composition and culture

- Effects on children's development of changes in family composition or structure (unresolved losses)
- Pressures associated with child's contact with non-resident parent
- Family beliefs, attitudes and rules about such issues as family membership, child-rearing, religion and punishments
- Influence of wider community and structural factors on family functioning (eg, income, employment, area of residence, housing, community resources)

Appendix 2

A model for analysing the impact of community on parents and children

In the separate poster available with this book we have produced a model which is based on the information and connections covered in the book. The aim of this model is to help practitioners when they think about the impact of community on children. In using this model the following points should be remembered.

- The model looks at strengths as well as pressures in local communities. There is a danger that workers focus disproportionately on pressures or deficiencies in communities.

- The term 'community' refers to all of the people the parents and child are in contact with outside their immediate or wider family. It can include communities of interest as well as geographical communities.

- The model incorporates 'hard' information (eg available facilities etc) and 'soft' information (eg parents' and children's perceptions of networks and perceptions of accessibility etc) to understand the impact of community.

- It is important that the definitions of 'community' should be those of the children and parents rather than professionals' definition of 'community' which are likely to be based on administrative boundaries.

- The model recognises the interactive nature of the impact of community on parents and children. The impact will be different for different children and parents depending on individual and family characteristics. Also of course children and parents will play their part in shaping their community.

- It is important to recognise that the impact of practical resources and network resources etc are cumulative and interactive. Different aspects of community should not be analysed in isolation.

Index of authors cited

A
Ahmad 117
Ainsworth 111, 113, 114, 118, 125, 134
Al Awad 109, 117
Aldgate 16, 28, 128, 135
Allan 129, 134
Amato 104, 118, 130, 134
Ammons 137
Anderson 131, 134
Ashworth 58, 67
Atherton 113, 119
Audit Commission 14, 28
Axinn 108, 120

B
Baker 128, 135
Baldry 37, 51
Baldwin 28, 34, 49
Ban 112, 119
Bandura 70, 81
Barn 12, 28
Barnat 30
Barnett 135
Beardsworth 123, 135
Becker 62, 66
Beckett 119
Beishon 129, 134
Belle 36, 49, 118, 119
Belsky 127, 137
Beresford 15, 28, 101, 102, 117, 135
Berridge 12, 30, 114, 117
Berthoud 57, 66, 88, 101, 102
Biehal 22, 28
Blackburn 89, 101
Bland 50, 66, 104, 108, 118
Blaxter 104, 117
Blehar 134

Booth 128, 130, 134
Bornat 51
Bowlby 124, 134
Bradley 126, 134
Braithwaite 58, 67
Brandon 136
Braunwald 135
Brisby 128, 135
Broad 113, 117
Bronfenbrenner 1, 7, 104, 108, 117
Brooks-Gunn 76, 81, 82, 84, 109
Brown 89, 101, 122, 135
Bryson 58, 59, 67
Bulkley 44, 49
Bullock 119
Burchinal 134
Burghes 130, 135
Burrows 13, 28, 87, 101
Buysse 43, 49
Byford 22, 28
Bywaters 30, 62, 67

C
Cain 119
Caldwell 134
Carlson 125, 135, 136
Carruthers 34, 49
Cartmel 74, 81
Caspi 76, 81, 126, 135
Cassell 128, 135
Chahal 79, 82
Chamba 110, 117, 123, 135
Chase-Lansdale 109, 117
Chess 123, 137
Child Poverty Action Group 61, 66
Cicchetti 135
Clark 62, 66, 99, 101
Clayden 22, 28

Cleaver 6, 7, 112, 113, 117, 128, 135
Cochran 43, 49, 74, 82
Cockett, 130, 135
Coleman 32, 49, 128, 135
Coll 134
Collins 137
Community Links 18, 28
Conger 76, 81, 82
Coohey 36, 49, 104, 117
Cooley 109, 120
Corwyn 134
Cotterill 33, 49
Coyne 121, 122, 136
Craig 57, 66
Crittenden 36, 49, 127, 135
Crnic 36, 52
Crouter 13, 29, 71, 82
Crow 110, 111, 112, 117, 129
Cumella 95, 102
Curtis 122, 135

D
Dadds 129, 135
Davey-Smith 30
David 51, 137
Davie 90, 101
Davies 97, 101
Davis 19, 28, 29, 41, 51, 62, 66
Day 22, 28
Daycare Trust 29, 58, 66, 72, 82
Dean 45, 49
Deater-Deckard 44, 49, 107, 117
Department for Work and Pensions 56, 57, 66

163

Department of Health 1, 7, 16, 31, 49, 63, 67, 73, 82, 83, 84, 85, 90, 98, 101, 122, 128, 135, 137, 148
Department of Social Security 72, 82
Department of Transport 28
DETR 11, 28
Dobson 57, 66, 123, 135
Dominelli 118
Dorling 30
Dowling 62, 66
Downes 46, 49
Downey 121, 122,135, 136
Duncan 76, 82, 84, 127, 137
Dunn 42, 107, 117, 126, 130, 136
Dunst 104, 118
Dyson 99, 101

E
Earls 32, 37, 51
Eiser 122, 131, 136
Elder 71, 76, 82, 127, 135
Entner Wright 81
Erooga 119
Eyers 19, 29

F
Families in Bayswater Bed and Breakfast 97, 101
Family Rights Group 111, 113, 118
Feather 70, 82
Feiring 40, 107, 118
Ferdinand 12, 28
Ferri 130, 136
Fineaman 70, 82
Fischer 32, 50, 74, 82, 103, 118
Ford 7, 83, 136
Fordham 87, 101
Forrest 86, 101
Fratter 114, 118
Freeman 20, 29, 112, 117

Fryer 70, 82
Furlong 74, 81
Furman 107, 118
Furstenberg 47, 50

G
Galambos 71, 83
Garbarino 13, 29, 37, 50
Gardner 34, 50
Garrett 114, 119
Gath 128, 136
Gaudin, 137
Ghate 16, 29
Gibbons 34, 50, 103, 104, 108, 118, 142, 151
Gilbert 22, 28
Gill 17, 29, 34, 39, 46, 50, 55, 59, 60, 66, 103, 104, 108, 118, 141, 148, 151
Giller 108, 119
Gilligan 5, 21, 29, 108, 118
Gilroy 9, 29, 33, 50
Goodman 56, 66
Gordon 12, 29, 30, 54,66
Greenberg 49
Gregg 58, 66
Grimshaw 15, 29
Guardian, The 29, 55, 62, 66, 72, 74, 75, 82, 105, 118, 148

H
H.M.Treasury 56, 62
Hagell 108, 119
Hamill 113, 118
Hargreaves 37, 51
Harkness 58, 66
Harris 89, 101, 122, 135
Hartley 70,83
Hartup 44, 50
Hashima 104, 118
Haskey 129, 136
Hayes 113, 117
Hazel 16, 29
Hedderwick 128, 135
Henderson 20, 28
Herbert 47, 51

Hillman 19, 29
Hills 87, 101
Hinde 135
Hinings, 136
Hirst 135
Holman 23, 24, 29, 142, 148
Horwath 5, 7, 118
Hosie 119
Howarth 67
Howe 45, 50, 125, 136
Howes 50
Hubbard 31, 51, 57, 67, 74, 83
Hundleby 114, 119
Hutchinson 101
Hutt 101

J
Jack 1, 2, 5, 7, 32, 33, 50, 73, 79, 82, 127, 132, 136
Jackson 111, 112, 118
Jacques 34, 50, 86, 102
Jahoda 70, 83
Jarrett 70, 83
Johnson 56, 66
Johnston 58, 67,75, 83
Jones 19, 29, 62, 67, 69, 78, 79, 83, 84, 124, 136, 141, 148
Jordan 139, 147, 148
Joseph Rowntree Foundation 51, 66, 67, 74, 77, 82, 84, 101, 102, 106, 118, 123, 136, 137

K
Kaufman 127, 136
Keane 119
Kelvin 70, 83
Kemp 87, 101
Kempson 18, 29, 58, 59, 67
Kendrick 21, 29
Kenway 67
Kettle 20, 28
Klebanov 76, 81, 84
Kupersmidt 45, 50

L
Lakey 88, 101
Land 19, 29
Lansley 54, 67
Lawton 117, 135
Lee 57, 67, 87, 101
Leet 104, 118
Lerner 71, 83
Lewis 40, 50, 107, 118, 141, 148
Lipsitt 83
Lister 62, 67
Little 119
Lloyd 15, 21, 29
Long 107, 119
Loughron 12, 29
Lucey 128, 135, 136, 137
Lupton 112, 118
Luster 83, 137
Lynd 71, 83

M
Maccoby 71, 83
Macdonald 15, 29, 67
Machin 58, 66
Mack 54, 67
Main 125, 127, 136
Maitland 22, 28
Malik 49
Malpass 87, 101
Maluccio 35, 50, 51, 111, 113, 114, 118
Manthorpe 57, 66
Marchant 79, 83
Marris 136
Marsh 110, 111, 112, 117, 118
Martin 71, 83
Mason 67, 83, 101
Mauthner, 78, 83
Maxwell 112.119
McAdoo 134
McGuire 15, 29, 42, 49
McHale 71, 82
McKee 78, 83
McLeod 62, 67
Melhuish 73, 83
Middleton 57, 58, 67, 123, 135
Millham 114, 115, 119
Millward 19, 29, 99, 101

Mistry 109, 119
Modood 88, 129, 134
Moffitt 81
Moncher 36, 50
Monk 108, 119
Morenoff 32, 37, 51
Morris 86, 112, 119
Morrison 119
Moss 21, 30, 73, 83
Murie 57, 67, 87, 101
Murray 58
Mussen 83

N
National Association of Citizens Advice Bureaux 67
National Centre for Social Research 105, 119
National Children's Home 83
Newman 28
Nixon 1111, 112, 118
Noble 57, 67, 79, 84
Novak 62, 67

O
Okagaki 82, 137
Oldman 98, 101, 102
Oliver 108, 119

P
Packman 34, 50, 86, 102
Palmer 67999
Pantazis 54, 66
Parke 45, 50
Parker 12, 29
Parkes 136
Parton 140, 148
Patterson 45, 50
Pavis 31, 51, 57, 67, 74, 83
Payne 70, 83
Pereira 30, 51
Petrie 21, 30
Piachaud 56, 67
Pilgrim 30, 51
Platt 74, 84, 89, 102
Plomin 126, 136
Poland 21, 30

Polansky 38, 51, 127, 137
Policy Studies Institute 78, 84
Porteous 22, 30
Porter 137
Power 96, 102
Prior 123, 137
Pritchard 21, 30
Pryor 130, 137
Pugh 16, 30
Puttnam 32, 51

Q
Qureshi 12, 30

R
Ragozin 49
Rahman 54, 67
Randall 34, 50, 86, 102
Reder 127, 128, 137
Reid 43,. 51
Reingold 75, 84
Repetti 71, 84
Richards 49
Ridge 28, 41, 51, 60, 67
Ridley 67, 83
Riecuiti 134
Riley 43, 49
Roberts 15, 30
Robins 121, 137
Robinson 49
Rock 44, 49
Rodgers 130, 137
Rolf 119
Rovee-Collier 83
Rowe 113, 114, 118, 119,
Rowlingson 58, 59, 67
Royal College of Physician 95, 102
Royal Society for the Prevention of Accidents 88, 102
Rugg 69, 78, 84
Rushforth 113, 117
Rutter 108, 119, 121, 123, 124, 137
Ryburn 110, 113, 119

S

Sage 129, 137
Sampson 32, 37, 51
Sapsford 118
Schofield 136
Schwartz 51
Select Committee on Social Security 55
Seligman 70, 84
Shaw 16, 25, 30
Shelter 85, 95, 96, 102
Sherman 37, 50
Shropshire 58, 67
Silva 81
Silverstein 107, 119
Simcha-Fagan 37, 51
Sinclair 16, 22, 30
Singh 126, 22, 30
Sloper 28
Smaje 57, 67
Smith 21, 30, 76, 84, 130, 136
Social Services Inspectorate 128, 137
Somerville 88, 102
Sonuga-Barke 109, 119
Speak 94, 102
Spencer 25, 30
St James-Roberts, I, 22, 30
Starr 35, 51
Statham 15, 16, 30
Stead 21, 29
Steele 88, 102
Steinberg 71, 84
Stepney 7, 83
Stevens 111, 118
Stevenson-Hinde 136
Stocker 43, 51
Stone 25, 30
Strell 78, 83
Stringer 49
Sulloway 128, 137
Sutherland 56, 67
Swain 112, 119
Sylva 21, 30

T

Tanner 66, 104, 108, 118
Thoburn 16, 30, 111, 113, 114, 118
Thomas 123, 137
Thompson 35, 38, 104, 119
Thornton 108, 120
Tietjen 106, 119
Tracey 35, 51
Tripp 130, 135
Trivette 104, 118

U

Unell 128, 135
Unger 109, 120
Uttal 106, 120

V

Vernon 21, 30
Vincent 101
Vinson 37, 51
Virdee 127, 129, 134
Vondra 127, 137
Vostanis 95, 102

W

Wall 134
Warr 70, 84
Waters 134
Watson 16, 30
Webb 56, 66
Webster 67, 83
Weiner 70, 84
Wellman 103, 120
Wenman 12, 30
Werner 21, 30, 32, 52, 108, 120
Wheway 19
White 131, 134
Whittaker 35
Whitty 96, 102
Whyley 18, 29
Wilding 16, 30
Wilkinson 67, 89, 102
Williams 9, 21, 30, 33, 51
Wilson 51
Winkley 15, 29
Winn 86, 102
Wortley 103, 120

Y

Yabiku 108, 120
Yeung 82
Yondell 96, 102

Z

Zamsky 109, 117
Zigler 127, 136